Perse Preparatory School.

For

R.A. c.1947.

"*Slaves filed in, bearing gold plates*"

NIKKAL SEYN

*A Tale of John Nicholson, Hero of Delhi,
Saviour of India*

by

ERNEST GRAY

Illustrated by DEREK EYLES

COLLINS
LONDON AND GLASGOW

PRINTED AND MADE IN GREAT BRITAIN BY
WM. COLLINS SONS AND CO. LTD.
LONDON AND GLASGOW

To

W. A. MULHOLLAND, M.C., B.A. (Cantab),
" Holly,"
wise and justly beloved schoolmaster,
to thank him for his gifts of *Chaucer* and *King
Solomon's Mines*, and the kindness he went
out of his way to show the author when
he was a very small and very shy schoolboy
at Cressbrook School, Kirkby Lonsdale.

CONTENTS

CHAP.   PAGE

I. MUD FORT OF CHITTAJEE   9

II. WRESTLING WITH DEV SAHAI   21

III. "WOLVES OF PATHANS"   39

IV. THE DEPUTY COMMISSIONER   55

V. A DUEL WITH BHANDARI   69

VI. THE JUDGMENT OF NIKKAL SEYN   83

VII. LION-HUNT   95

VIII. THE RAJAH ENTERTAINS   109

IX. THE BROKEN TWIG   125

X. THE SWORD AND THE BIBLE   137

XI. HYMN TO NIKKAL SEYN   153

XII. SURGERY IN A FROCK-COAT   159

XIII. ENCOUNTER WITH THE PATHANS   169

XIV. MUTINY!   179

XV. THE CAPTURE OF DELHI   195

XVI. "SUCH A FIGHT!"   205

XVII. "TILL DELHI IS TAKEN!"   223

Chapter One

MUD FORT OF CHITTAJEE

THE mud fort of Chittajee, perched on a crag between two spurs of the vast mountain ranges dividing the Punjab from Afghanistan, brooded in silence beneath the blazing afternoon sun. Nothing stirred in the dusty barrack square, the ensign hung limp against its staff; except for a perspiring sentry on the rough wooden watch-tower, the temporary garrison of a detachment of the Eighty-seventh Regiment of Foot[1] had all sought shelter within doors.

Suddenly the sentry, who had idly watched a knot of vultures drift slowly up the valley towards the gates, gave a hoarse shout.

In the guard-room, Richard Marvel, drummer boy—usually known as Lanky Dick, or "the Dicky Bird," from his shrill piping voice—awoke with a yell as a heavy boot flew through the air and struck his head smartly.

"Is ut dramin' again ye are, Marvel?" cried Corporal Green. "Niver did Oi see such a marvel of a bhoy for sleep! Be up with you, and sound y'r drum—the Lieutenant's back!"

Rubbing his bristly head ruefully, Dick pulled the slings of his drum over his thin shoulders and ran

[1] Now better known as the Royal Irish Fusiliers (87th Princess Victoria's) —*Author.*

11

out after the guard. The stirring roll of the Assembly echoed defiantly among the hills as the gates were opened and a weary little procession straggled in.

First came Lieutenant Close, on foot, leading his mountain pony, on which swayed a wounded infantryman in a scarlet coat with the blue regimental facings. Two more red-coats followed, bearing a fourth soldier on their muskets. A fifth infantryman dragged along a struggling native, whose fierce tawny eyes and ruffled robes made him resemble some captive bird of prey. The uniforms of all were white with dust and stained by blood and sweat.

"They've only been out an hour," Dick heard a whisper from the ranks behind. "Where's Frank Shepherd?"

"Stop that talking in the ranks!" cried the officer hoarsely. "Colour Sergeant, what is that drummer boy doing without his cap? Does the fool want to catch sunstroke?"

Dick burst into a prickly heat of embarrassment. He was always in trouble, and now he would catch it for certain. What had he been thinking of, to forget his cap with its protective linen back flap? But as the Sergeant bore down on him, an ominous gleam in his eye, a fat man appeared on the veranda of the officers' quarters.

"What has happened, Lieutenant?" he cried anxiously. "You have been fired upon, I see!"

"We were ambushed a few miles down the valley,"

returned the Lieutenant. "Come inside and I will tell you all about it!"

At that instant a puff of white smoke rose lazily among the rocks on the nearest hill-side. The flag jerked sharply, and the sentry in the tower dropped his musket with a loud clatter into the barrack square. Then he reeled drunkenly, swayed for one moment at the rail, and collapsed on the tower floor.

As if his action was a signal, a dozen more white puffs rose above the rocks. Heavy lead balls hummed through the air high overhead, or struck the mud walls with a thud and spurt of dust.

"Beat the Rally, drummer!" cried the Lieutenant. "Every man to the walls! Sergeant, issue each man with a bottle of water and forty rounds of ammunition!"

The fat man, Mr. Malcolm Thomas by name, an official of the East India Company, mopped his face with an enormous blue silk handkerchief.

"What are you going to do with your prisoner, Close?" he asked.

"Hang him, as a warning to his friends out there," came the grim reply.

"Oh, come now, let's not be hasty," began the fat man hurriedly. "There must be an inquiry—the Deputy Commissioner——"

Through the roll of his drum Dicky heard the Lieutenant reply:

"Three white soldiers have been killed and these natives must be taught to respect our uniform. As

Captain Baxter is dying of fever, I am the military commander here, and you must allow me to use my own judgment. When we have executed that ruffian, we must retire at once to the Punjab—we can't hold out here—and I only hope some of us get back alive!"

And he stalked away to shout orders at the rest of the garrison, who were hastily turning out, while Mr. Thomas shook his head dismally and turned back into the mess.

"'Tis lucky for you I've a kind hearrt, ye iverlastin' disgrace," growled the Colour Sergeant, jamming on Dicky's head a cap, far too large for it, that a grinning infantryman proffered. "To-night you and I will have a little tark! Hi, stop that man, ye crazy omadhauns!"

For as the gates creaked shut, the native prisoner took advantage of the confusion to wrench himself free, darted between the gates, and vanished outside.

In vain the Lieutenant shouted orders. The native had disappeared among the rocks by the winding path where an hour later the garrison filed down into the valley.

They numbered only a score, lighting the stores, ammunition, arms, and furniture they could not carry away as funeral pyre over four of the detachment who had been killed.

Lieutenant Close marched grimly at the head, with Dick beside him beating the "Rally." The Lieutenant's pony, and that of Mr. Thomas, had been harnessed to a rough cart, half a sledge, on which lay the wasted figure of Captain Baxter and two wounded red-coats. Mr. Thomas, pistol in hand, walked beside the Captain, whilst the scowling, bearded Colour Sergeant, furled ensign over his shoulder, brought up the rear. The men formed round them, three paces between each, and with faces set to the safety of the distant Punjab, they struggled on under the pitiless sun and a hail of lead, clay balls propelled from slings, and even spears and stones, from the shouting tribesmen dodging over the hill slopes.

"The walls of the fort would have afforded more —ahem!—shelter," observed Mr. Thomas, walking up beside the Lieutenant.

"Oh, we should have been quite safe—until our ammunition and water gave out!" retorted the officer sarcastically.

"Ah, yes ; quite so." The fat man took careful aim at a native waving derisive arms from a crag. "The Deputy Commissioner will be furious," he added with a sigh, blowing away the smoke curling round the pistol muzzle.

The Lieutenant muttered angrily in his beard.

"Who is this Deputy Commissioner?" he demanded in exasperated tones. "All you fellows seem terrified of him!"

"I was forgetting you were new to this section." Mr. Thomas reloaded his pistol. "Mr. John Nicholson, you will find, is a person to be reckoned with. In only four years he has brought peace to the Punjab, once the most lawless province in India!"

"Not *the* John Nicholson, the wild fighter of the last Sikh war seven years ago, in 1849?"

"The same man," nodded Mr. Thomas.

"Why, of course I've heard of him! Who has not?"

The Lieutenant glanced sharply at Dicky, whose monotonous roll had begun to stammer. "Your arms getting tired, youngster? Give me the drum!"

"I'm all right, sir," said Dicky in an agitated squeak. "It is jolly hot, though, isn't it?" he added, half to himself, and then blushed crimson at his presumption.

But the Lieutenant ignored it.

"Hand the drum over, boy!" he said. "Get a musket if you want to be useful!"

Taking the slings from Dick's sticky paws, he observed over his shoulder to Mr. Thomas : "This is the spot where we were ambushed earlier in the afternoon! See how the crags loom over the road? Poor Shepherd went off his head, and ran up the rocks with his bayonet before I could stop him. Can you get back and watch the rear?"

Nodding his heavy head, his four chins disappearing into two as he set his jaw, Mr. Thomas waved his hand, and turned back, while Dick, with a start, saw James Burt, who walked just behind him, sway and fall to his knees.

"Oh, lor'!" said Dick shrilly. "P-please, Mr. Burt, can I help you?"

"'Tis me shoulder," replied the soldier hoarsely. "Prop me up, Dicky, and then take a sight with my gun at yon screeching devil capering on that rock! Ah, that's right!"

The musket went off with a bang. Powder blackened Dick's face, whilst the recoil of the heavy piece almost knocked him flat. But the native fell down with a yell, and, dropping the gun, Dick regained his balance, painfully propping up the infantryman, whose blood was oozing thickly over Dick's own coat.

Natives seemed to be all about them now. Dicky was deafened by their screams, whilst choking powder smoke almost blinded him. But dimly he could see the familiar red-coats all about, whilst the rattle of the drum beat staccato through the din. Private Burt was slipping to his knees again, and it took all the strength of Dicky's weedy form to support him.

Somehow he managed to drag him beneath the shelter of an overhanging rock, and knelt down beside him, pulling out his water-bottle, and attempting to force some of its contents through the soldier's clenched teeth.

"I'm done for, Dicky!" Burt stirred abruptly. "Get back to the others, or they'll get you too!" He lifted a limp hand, then sighed.

"Mr. Burt! Please——" began Dicky, his voice

more shrill than ever, "have another drink—Mr. Burt?"

But Private James Burt was dead, and Dicky slowly laid his head down in the dust, acutely aware that his left arm was numb with the soldier's weight.

The din of combat, which had roared, echoing beneath the crags, seemed now to be dying away. Dicky threw himself flat in the shadows as a dancing native, flourishing a tulwar whose steel was dulled with black stains, whirled madly up the road, slashing at Private Burt's body. Two more natives followed, screaming with savage rage as a crash of musketry fire again shattered the dust-filled air.

Dicky, scared and bewildered, carefully raised his head. Evidently he was cut off from his comrades, but it occurred to him he might be able to join them over the top of the rocks. Jumping to his feet, he scrambled madly up the cliff face, indifferent to what he might find at the top so long as he got away from the savage with the tulwar. Up and up he went, pebbles and earth flying beneath his heavy boots, hand over fist till he lay panting on a broad shelf of sun-baked stone. There he paused to listen, one ear cocked for sounds above, one bent down to listen to the fading sounds of the fight along the road.

The defiant rattle of the drum had ceased, and as the dust and smoke settled, Dick could see the white ribbon of the road below. It was dotted by two or three red-coated and white-robed figures, the bodies of his friends and their assailants; about a quarter of a mile away the road vanished round another huge mass of brown rocks, and Dick thought he could see his drum lying at their foot.

But there was no sign of the column, and shouting hillmen were scurrying out like ants from behind the rocks, and he had no desire at all to be spotted by that horrible lunatic with the blood-stained sword.

Turning, he scrambled on despairingly, till at length he crawled on to a flat plateau at the summit where the full blast of the sun struck him like a blow. Breathless, aching in every limb, trembling with fright, he crawled on cautiously to the shelter of a near-by clump of withered bushes. Every second he expected to hear a yell of discovery from the natives, or feel a bullet thump into his back, but those hillmen nearest to him were intent only on swarming into the ravine to loot their victims. His cap kept falling over his nose, his hands were torn and bleeding, his clumsy boots felt as heavy as six-pound shot; but somehow he managed to reach the precious shelter, and dragged himself, panting, into the very centre of the bushes. There he promptly fell fast asleep.

Chapter Two

WRESTLING WITH DEV SAHAI

WHEN he awoke it was night. The air was still and cold, and over the mountains hung a crescent moon, outlining in black relief the still smoking fort on its lofty crag. In the distance a jackal barked.

Dick felt sore all over, and terribly thirsty, but when he lifted his water-bottle to his lips found it almost empty. He sucked down the few remaining drops greedily, dismally reminded by his action of poor Private Burt, and all his other comrades, who now lay stiff and lifeless in the valley. Though often their butt, poor Dicky had never found their rough jokes malicious or deliberately brutal, and some tears came into his eyes, which he wiped away with a sniffle. What would he not give to be back in camp —even with a beating ahead from the Colour Sergeant—even though Private Miles, that practical joker, filled his cap again with red ants? Where was he to go now? Impossible to stay until dawn revealed his red-coat to the lynx eyes of the prowling hillmen.

With another despairing sniffle he crawled out of the bushes, and a shadow flitted over the rocks.

"O, son of a Pandi!" said a strange voice softly. "Stand forth and stretch out thy hands, that I may see they conceal no weapon!"

Dick knew nothing of the Indian native dialect, but the ominous click-clock! of a cocked pistol that accompanied the words was unmistakable.

Firmly convinced that that revolting object with the sword had been patiently waiting for him to appear, and that this was his last moment on earth, a strange mixture of terror, rage, and pity for his dead comrades suddenly boiled up inside Dicky. He hurtled forward, his fingers clutched the cloth of a robe, he had one glimpse against the stars of a hook nose, of an arm raised to strike . . .

"Ah, wait, Syed!" whispered a second voice urgently. "See, 'tis a young feringhee soldier!"

Iron fingers released their painful grip of Dick's bony shoulder, and, dizzy and confused, he shambled to his feet.

"Make no noise, soldier," warned the second voice in English. "We are friends!"

"Then why wave a pistol at me?" demanded Dicky shrilly.

"Psst!" said the first voice angrily. "The fool chatters like a monkey!"

"Be quiet," said the second voice in English; "your life depends upon your silence. Follow us, and we will take you to your friends!"

Dicky scratched his head and stared at the two dim figures standing motionless in the gloom. One was shorter than the other, and both were dressed in long dark robes with hoods drawn over their heads and across the lower part of their faces, so that he could see only the glitter of their eyes. The bright moonlight glinted also on the barrel of the pistol which the first and taller figure still held in his hand,

and the more Dicky stared at the pair the less he liked the look of them.

But he was unarmed, and no physical match at least for Syed. He shrugged his shoulders, and the shorter figure turned and led the way down towards the ravine, Dicky uneasily conscious of the second soundless figure that trod on his heels.

On the valley road the leader strode off towards the south-east, his back to the fort. " So far so good," thought Dicky. "This is my way, and perhaps I can give them the slip later."

A strange but familiar odour crept into his nose— the unmistakable smell of camel. Where the road left the hills and plunged down into open country, Dicky saw a caravan drawn up in silence. A third silent figure flitted across to bar their path; a few muttered words, and Syed thrust his pistol into Dicky's ribs, motioning him towards a black mass which, on close inspection, revealed itself to be a squatting camel with a heavy load on its back.

When dawn broke, Dicky found himself far from that ghastly gorge, tramping along in rear of the caravan, with the watchful Seyd at his side.

The second cowled figure had disappeared, but as Dick, weary and thirsty, stooped to take a pebble out of his boot-top, a gay voice hailed him from top of the rugs piled on the camel he was patiently following.

Dick looked up, and squeaked indignantly as he saw what dangled beside the rugs.

'You've got my drum!" he said, rubbing his eyes.

"Your drum?" asked his captor. "How can it be that, when we found it in the valley?"

With a grin revealing white even teeth, a tall youth of about Dicky's age slipped from the rugs to his side.

"It belongs to the regiment," said Dicky. "There'll be a terrible row when the Colonel finds you've——"

"Do not say what I think is on your tongue." The youth drew himself sternly erect. "We are not robbers, but shall we refuse what Allah offers?"

This remark confused Dicky, but he tried gamely to stick to the point.

"All the same it's my drum," he said, his voice rising higher and higher in indignation. "Why, I used to play on it!"

"But now it is yours no longer." With a wave of a slender brown hand the youth dismissed the subject. "Tell me, how many feringhee soldiers were in your troop? And how did you come to be on top of the cliff?"

"I'm not telling you anything," said Dicky shrilly. "And that's still my drum!"

"You are ungrateful," retorted the youth. "If we had not rescued you, the Pandis would by now be tearing your bones from their sockets!"

"Oh, well," said Dicky, pricked by remorse, "I'm sorry—I really am. What's your name? You speak English jolly well!"

"I am Dev Sahai, and this is the caravan of my

father, Yusuf Khan Sahai, who awaits us in Peshawar.
He does not speak your tongue, for he is of the old
faith, but his brother, Zafar, my uncle, who now
leads the caravan, was once Jemadar[1] in a sepoy
regiment. From him I have learnt to speak English,
learning more of it from others, for it is a very
useful thing to know. Moreover, I can speak for my
people in his own tongue to the great Nikkal Seyn!"
and he salaamed.

"Who's him?" asked Dicky ungrammatically.

"You, a feringhee, and a soldier, ask me that?
Nikkal Seyn is the Commissioner of your mighty
East Indian Company, a giant whose shadow covers
the earth, at whose step the wicked shiver; a just
man, a strong man, a terrible man, but our friend,
the friend of all who strive to walk in peace and
righteousness!"

"Oh, you mean John Nicholson," said Dicky,
rather overwhelmed by this description of a man
who was to him, as yet, only a name.

The youth nodded.

"Even so, Nikkal Seyn, as I have said. Because
he is our friend, and because his eye spies out the
evildoer, we stopped as we came down the gorge,
beholding the bodies of your soldiers, and the gifts
which perhaps Allah had left us after the savage
Pandis had taken their pick. They are crows and
jackals," the youth went on bitterly, "insulting
Allah, for which they shall surely pay!"

[1] A native lieutenant—*Author*.

"In what way?" asked Dicky, puzzled.

"They had looted all save yonder drum, the top of which they had broken in. Therefore I and Syed Ali, who is my guard, climbed to the cliff top, but found naught. But as we turned away, Syed heard you moving in the bushes, and the rest you know!"

Even to Dicky, used to the eternal "scrounging" of army life, it seemed his saviours had unusual ideas about other people's property. But he thought it unwise to say so, and so he began chatting away to Dev, asking him his age—the Indian was just turned sixteen, two years older than himself—and telling him artlessly how he had not been long in India, having joined the regiment at Allahabad eighteen months before.

After a few more miles he began to wonder when they were going to breakfast, but Dev only laughed at his question.

"We feed at the cool of sun-down. But if you are thirsty, I have a drink here, somewhat like that the feringhees call ghee!"

And he proffered a goatskin flask, which Dick found to contain a weird mixture of sour milk and rancid butter. But as nothing better was available, he swallowed a few mouthfuls with a wry face.

"I must now leave you," said Dev. "To-night, when we pitch camp, I will visit you again!"

"Lor'," said Dicky in shrill alarm, "won't I be murdered?"

"Only if you try to run away," smiled Dev, a

reply that did not altogether please Dicky. However, Syed had walked away, and after a long look back at the menacing mountains, now some distance behind, Dicky unbuttoned the neck of his jacket and plodded on after the camel.

Eighteen months of marching over India, from Bombay to Hyderabad, from Hyderabad across the United Provinces to the Khymur Hills and so to Allahabad, had seasoned Dicky, and he felt no particular discomfort as the hours passed and the sun rose to its zenith and then slowly dropped to-wards the western horizon. He was grateful for the shade cast by the camel and its load, and tramped on in the dust, listening to the steady rhythmic padding of the beast's splay feet, to the jingle of the caravan bells, the cries of the camel-drivers, and the endless quavering song of a strolling musician somewhere just ahead.

Everyone seemed very glad to be out of the hills, and as they fell away into the horizon, the natives laughed and cracked jokes, pointing back to the mountains and gesticulating and pulling faces.

Towards dusk the caravan halted beside a deserted house, and those members of the caravan who were Mohammedans pulled out small praying-mats and fell upon their knees. Behind them the camp servants lit fires of camel dung, and set great pots simmering.

Dicky sat down thankfully against the load he had been following all day whilst the camel was led away to be watered at a near-by spring. The drum was also carried away, and Dicky did not expect to see it again. Syed strode up to him with a bowl containing dates and a stew of goat flesh, and Dicky, who felt famished, set to work with a will. There were chupattis,[1] or baked cakes, and milk also, and after he had eaten everything edible within reach he felt a great deal better. But the nights are cold in India, and he got up, intending to stroll over to one of the camp fires, when once more Syed appeared, and made signs he was to follow him.

Feeling a little uneasy, Dicky did so, and was led by his guide to the courtyard of the house.

There he found Dev squatting upon a brightly coloured rug, beside him a burly native whose face was almost completely hidden behind a great black beard which flowed down to his knees; wearing a red and blue robe, with pointed yellow slippers and a silk turban, he sat placidly sucking at a hookah, the smoke bubbling through rose-water. From the shadows behind came the shrill music of native pipes.

Dev looked up and smiled, and the burly native lifted the mouthpiece of the hookah from his lips to observe in a deep rumbling voice:

"Welcome, young stranger, to the caravan of Yusuf Khan Safai. Be seated." And he clapped his hands.

As Dicky squatted down beside Dev, who was arrayed in a flowing blue robe, embroidered with

---

[1] Unleavened cakes—*Author*.

pearls and gold thread, silent servants handed him a tiny silver cup containing sherbet.

"Let us drink to Allah, Preserver of all," said the burly stranger, picking up a similar cup from the rug, "who has rescued an innocent lamb from the wiles of the jackal!"

Dicky thought it would be unkind not to respond to the thought behind the words, even though he was not, of course, a Mussulman, and so lifted his cup of sherbet solemnly, and drank it off.

"I noted from the numbers on their collars that your dead comrades were of the 87th Regiment of Foot," went on the burly man. "I, Zafar Muhamed Safai, was once jemadar in the Third Regiment of Native Horse. Therefore my heart bleeds with yours, young stranger, for those who have been carried to their fathers. But they shall be avenged! Surely Allah, whose ways are inscrutable, has smitten those dogs of Pandis with madness to their undoing, for this is the country ruled by Nikkal Seyn, the mighty one, the tramp of whose war horse is heard from Attock to the Khyber! He will hark to the cry of the murdered ones, and exact a just and terrible vengeance!"

"You speak truly, oh Zafar Muhamed Safai!" said a musical voice.

"Nikkal Seyn! 'Tis Nikkal Seyn!" and the burly man jumped to his feet, and salaamed, knocking his forehead against the ground, while Dev followed his example, and a great welcoming roar swept over the camp and men came swarming to the courtyard gates.

Into the flickering firelight stepped a tall man dressed in grey trousers and a grey, semi-military frock-coat, with a broad pale blue sash swathed round his waist and a loose black stock wound round his muscular throat. From all he had heard of him, Dicky had imagined the famous John Nicholson to resemble some craggy prize-fighter, but the new-comer was as graceful as a mountain ash. Long glossy black hair fell to his shoulders; his eyes were dark and sparkling, and beneath an aquiline nose the points of a sweeping black moustache ran into a thick spade-shaped beard. His forehead was white and lofty. The grey frock-coat strained over a chest like a barrel, and its sleeves were taut over the rippling arm muscles. His hands and feet, though sinewy, were narrow and small. Fingers crossed over the hilt of a curved sword, whose scabbard was of white leather inlaid with gold, he stood and smiled in the dusk.

Then his eyes fell upon Dicky, and at once his whole expression changed.

"What are you doing here?" he asked Dicky coldly. "You are a drummer of the Eighty-seventh Foot, are you not?"

"We rescued the youth only last night, lord," said Zafar Sahai, rising to his feet with another profound salaam. "He was hiding from the wicked tribesmen who attacked his detachment!"

"Where is your drum?" asked John Nicholson sternly.

"P-please, sir," said Dicky, rubbing one boot against the other, "the Lieutenant took it from me, but——"

"Lieutenant Close?"

"Y-yes, sir!"

"Go on!"

"Lieutenant Close took it from me, and then we were attacked and Mr.-Private-Burt was shot, and I gave him some water, and then I got lost, and climbed a cliff and went to sleep in some bushes!"

"Lieutenant Close is now lying seriously wounded at Peshawar. I hope for his sake and that of the honour of your regiment you are telling the truth. You should not have lost your drum. Have you any idea where it may be?"

"P-please, sir," said Dicky desperately, "he's got it!" indicating Dev.

"My nephew found it in a valley a day's march from here," interposed Zafar Sahai smoothly.

"Then you should have got it back, boy. What is your name?"

"Richard Marvel, sir!"

John Nicholson frowned thoughtfully at the fire. Then he spoke rapidly in native dialect to Zafar, who first looked glum, and then burst into a rich bellow of appreciative laughter, shaking his head in agreement, and tucking his thumbs into his sash.

"Your rescuers believe in the adage 'findings are

keepings,' Marvel," said John Nicholson. "Dev Sahai found the drum, but you have lost property of the Company which was entrusted to you! Are you game to wrestle with Dev for it? Don't use your fists—to strike him would be a mortal insult!"

"Me fight him?" said Dick shrilly, and eyed Dev's sinewy form uneasily. "Why—yes, sir!"

Zafar stretched out his great arms.

"Hearken, all ye folk, to the wisdom and justice of Nikkal Seyn! My nephew has a drum which this young feringhee says is his. Therefore, says Nikkal Seyn, let Allah decide the issue!"

Grinning and chattering, the camel-drivers and guards formed a rough circle outside the gates of the courtyard, whilst Dev, with a flash of white teeth, stripped to the waist, and stood up lithe and strong in a pair of loose baggy trousers caught round his ankles. As Dick, feeling more and more nervous, took off his coat, and slowly rolled up the sleeves of his rough grey shirt, Dev began circling round and round him, arms outstretched, fingers hooking the air, a wicked light in his merry brown eyes.

"Take off thy boots, feringhee," Safar bent to whisper in Dick's ear. "They are heavy, and may slip in the dust!"

So Dicky removed his clumsy boots, and feeling remarkably like a new plucked chicken, stood up and threw back his head.

At once Dev bounded at him, and kicked him

heavily with both feet in the stomach. Startled and bewildered, Dicky stumbled back, and Dev threw his arms round him, and bit his ear savagely.

This was too much for Dicky. With a yell of mingled rage and pain, he tore the native boy from him, tripped, and fell heavily on top of him.

A roar of delight and surprise went up from the watching circle, but poor Dicky's weedy form could not hold Dev, who wriggled and plunged like a captive snake. In vain Dicky, his mouth and nose full of dust, strove to grab one of the arms and legs flying past him. He was jerked on to his back, and Dev leapt like a young panther on to his narrow chest, pressing his shoulders down into the ground.

At once he sprang to his feet, leaving Dicky to scramble awkwardly to his own legs.

"Allah has spoken," said Zafar Sahai solemnly. "The drum is ours!"

He threw a massive arm round each of the boy's shoulders.

"Now shake hands, English fashion, and kiss each other, as is our custom, and you are friends for ever!"

Dicky shyly held out his hand. Dev clasped it warmly, and with an answering smile kissed him lightly on the cheek. Then he beckoned to a servant, who brought them another cup of sherbet, from which they both drank.

"Bad luck, Marvel," said John Nicholson, stepping

forward. "But you did your best, and nobody can do more!"

"He's got funny ideas about wrestling, sir," piped Dick, tenderly massaging his ear.

"Yes, this is India, Marvel, not the playground of an English school. But Dev and his family are your friends now, and will never betray or harm you, either by word or deed!"

As Dicky sat down and began lacing up his boots, Zafar approached, and with a low salaam inquired of Nicholson, "Do you honour us with your company to-night, Lord?"

John Nicholson nodded.

"There is a blanket strapped to my saddle on which I will sleep here until dawn. Then I must depart!"

Zafar strode away, shouting orders, and Nicholson sat down beside Dick on the rug.

"Would you recognise the native prisoner who escaped from the fort?"

It struck Dicky that the great man had an astonishing knowledge of all that had gone on, but Nicholson, noting the surprise in his face, chuckled softly.

"I met your men two miles from Peshawar, and Mr. Thomas told me what had happened!"

"I think I would know him again, sir," said Dicky. "He had a scar near his right ear! Why, are you going back into the hills, sir?"

"Yes, Marvel, I am, and as you can identify this gentleman, I want you to come with me!"

"Me, sir!" shrilled Dicky, staring at Nicholson. But the protest on his lips died away. There was something hypnotic in the steady gaze that met his. "Oh, very well, sir! When do we start?"

"At daybreak," said John Nicholson, and got up and walked away to where his blanket had been spread beneath the shade of the ruined wall.

Chapter Three

"WOLVES OF PATHANS"

When the sun rose into the sky next morning, it found Dicky and John Nicholson already approaching the foothills. Nicholson led the way on a magnificent black charger whose harness was of white leather embroidered with silver. Dick struggled after on a tiny mountain pony whose ribs chafed his knees. He had never ridden before, but he was grimly determined to stick on somehow. Rising before dawn, when thick cold mists veiled the country-side, they had swallowed a mouthful of coffee and goat's meat, and ridden back along the road amid the good wishes of Dev and Zafar, and the low salaams of the camel drivers and guards. It was as well perhaps that Dicky was so engrossed in sticking on to his mountain pony. He had no time to worry about what might happen when they got back to that dreadful gloomy gorge.

On they rode, Nicholson glancing back now and again at Dicky, and smiling quietly to himself at his efforts to urge his pony forward. The sun rose still higher into the brazen vault of heaven, the occasional piping note of a bird ceased, and with a thrill of horror Dicky, looking up, saw a thick cluster of vultures hovering over the road ahead.

Before noon they were entering the ravine, and Dicky tried to keep his eyes between his pony's ears, so that he should not see the horrid sights strewn along the valley. Vultures and jackals had torn the bodies in pieces, bones and fragments of clothing were strewn everywhere in the dust, whilst a sickly smell filled the air. Round their heads swooped the vultures, their huge wings rustling in slow sweeps.

But no shot greeted them, not a tribesman was visible, and John Nicholson rode on steadily, and led the way up the path and into the ruined fort, the gates of which had been dragged from their hinges. It was completely gutted, and some attempt had been made to drag the six-pound brass cannon set at the foot of the watch-tower down to the valley. Its carriage stood by the gates, whilst the barrel lay on the ground half a dozen feet away.

Dismounting, and tying his horse to a post, John Nicholson strode over and inspected the gun.

"Why, there is still a charge in it!" he exclaimed. "Get that handspike by the wall there, Marvel! We'll mount the piece again!"

Dicky was so stiff that at first his legs wandered in circles. But he did as he was ordered, and setting the handspike beneath the barrel, waited whilst Nicholson ran the carriage alongside. Then he leant all his weight on the lever, allowing Nicholson, who had removed his coat, to get his hands beneath the ponderous cylinder. A heave, a breathless pause, then with a gasp and a quiet laugh, John Nicholson had swung the gun back on to the carriage. Dicky stood blinking at him in amazement, struck dumb by his enormous strength, starting violently as Nicholson said crisply, "Set the handspike under the carriage and push the gun to the gates!" and slipped on his coat again.

"Now, Marvel," he said, when the cannon was in position, "we will summon the congregation!"

"But where are they, sir?" asked Dicky.

"Everywhere around us," came the reply. "We have been closely watched ever since we entered that blood-stained gorge!"

A chill crept up Dicky's spine as he peered out through the ruined gates at the empty hills. Only the vultures wheeled and circled above the rocks, but if what John Nicholson said was true——

"Stand clear, Marvel!" cried Nicholson. "When I've fired the charge, I shall climb up there," and he pointed to the parapet over the gate. "You stand in the shadow here, with this pistol, in case there's any nonsense!"

To say Dicky was scared was to describe his feelings mildly. He had a sudden memory of the dancing maniac with the sword, and here they were, two solitary white men, who had deliberately ridden into the very heart of a lonely countryside filled with savages thirsting for white men's blood. Trembling, with a dry mouth, he took the proffered pistol, and stepped aside.

John Nicholson struck a light, and the gun went off with a roar and belched clouds of thick white smoke.

Instantly there was a wild clamour from every hill slope, a fierce screaming and yelling that beat against the shattered walls like the waves of the sea. From right and from left, up from the valley and across from the rocks, bearded, hook-nosed tribesmen poured towards the crag; a wave of brandished lance points, of swords and muskets tossed in the air; shouting defiance at the solitary figure standing outlined against the sky. Up the path they rushed, until the foremost were only three hundred odd yards from the gates, and it seemed to Dicky that all was lost.

But something ominous in the stillness of the figure watching them from the parapet daunted the first ranks. Their shouts died away; they dropped to a run, to a walk.

"Death to the feringhee!" screamed some.

"Aye, but see you not it is Nikkal Seyn?" cried back others.

Suddenly Nicholson threw out his arms.

"Stop!" he cried in a voice like thunder. "Let only your chiefs come forward to the gates!"

He spoke in Pahari, the hill dialects, and there was a wondering murmur from the tribesmen. They swayed and eddied a moment, then the press parted, and two tall chieftains stepped forward.

"What does Nikkal Seyn require of us?" cried one insolently.

"Justice," returned Nicholson grimly. "A party of white soldiers lately came into your hills, seeking your friendship. But you fired upon them, killing seven. Therefore, he that led those that murdered the feringhees must die. His doom is decreed by your own law of hospitality, as well as by my justice, the justice of Nikkal Seyn, servant of John Company! Bring forth this man, therefore, and depart to your villages!"

"The reign of the British Raj shall be a hundred years. So says the prophecy," returned the second chief. "By the battle at Plassey the feringhees conquered the soft people of the plains, but now the hundred years have run, and we but light the fire that shall burn them out!"

"Plassey was fought in the year 1757. This is the year 1856," said Nicholson. "Ye have attacked too soon, and therefore offend the gods!"

There was consternation among the tribesmen, and the two chiefs turned and stared at each other in dismay.

"How do we know ye speak truth?" cried the first anxiously.

"My word is my bond!" said Nicholson simply. He folded his arms and watched as a noisy discussion, with much waving of arms, broke out. After some minutes the two chiefs turned on their heels, and went back into the mob, returning with three or four tribesmen who dragged along between them a struggling native.

"O, Nikkal Seyn," cried the first chief, "it is known to all men ye never tell a lie! Therefore we deliver up to you he who led the band that attacked the feringhees. What is the doom ye decree? Shall he be slashed in pieces, burnt with hot irons, trampled beneath the hooves of your mighty charger?"

"Marvel," said John Nicholson, "is this the man who was captured?"

Dicky edged nervously out into the sunlight, and stared at the struggling hillman who snarled at him like a wild beast. White against the brown skin ran the scar of an old sword cut on the temple.

"P-please, sir, I think so, sir—yes, sir!"

"Hang the evil-doer to yonder flag staff!" cried John Nicholson. "Leave him to swing, that all who live in the hills may respect the word of Nikkal Seyn and the law of the great White Queen!"

Late that night, Dicky sat with John Nicholson in the house of a village headman. Nicholson had ridden out from the fort through the staring ranks of the hillmen, and turned his horse, not to the Punjab, but into the mountain defiles, visiting, during the afternoon, four widely scattered villages, lying south, east, north, and west of the ruined fort. At each village he had called the natives together, and given to the headman a piece of the turban of the executed native, as a sign they were to respect the white man's law.

The village in the west was not reached until the sun was setting behind the snow-capped ranges, and Dicky was nearly exhausted. But although they were scores of miles away from camp, surrounded by savage, ignorant natives, he had realised how powerful was the aura of mystery and fear that surrounded his companion. Therefore he sat by the fire, munching chupattis, quite unruffled by his strange position, and conscious of a growing love and admiration for Nicholson's magnetic personality.

John Nicholson himself was lying on his blankets with his hands clasped behind his head, staring dreamily into the fire. They were quite alone, though on the other side of the wall Nicholson's charger rustled drowsily in his straw, and from far away an owl hooted.

"Marvel," said Nicholson, "you don't talk quite like an ordinary drummer boy. Who were your parents?"

"Please, sir," said Dicky, taking a deep breath, "father was master at a penny school at Paddington, but he died before I was born, and mother died four years after she married again, when I was five, and stepfather, who was a law-writer in Little Paul's Yard, brought me up and was going to put me in his shop, only on my tenth birthday I upset a bottle of ink all over some very important documents he was engrossing, and he was so annoyed he kicked me out!"

John Nicholson smiled, and raised himself on one elbow.

"Very unfortunate! What did you do then?"

"Well, sir, Mr. Pyke—stepfather, that was—was

always talking about the East India Company, saying what a wonderful thing it was that a private company should own a huge rich country the size of Europe, and how he wished he had some shares in it. So I went down to the East India House, only on the way I met a sergeant who asked me if I wanted to go to India, and when I did, said he'd get me there for nothing if I'd just wear a red coat. And as I said I hadn't any money, he said how lucky it was he'd met me, and so I became a drummer boy!"

"But do you want to be a drummer boy all your life, or to try and get into the Company?"

"Please, sir, I'd sooner join the Company!"

"Well, Marvel," said Nicholson slowly, "you have been a good orderly to-day, obeying orders swiftly and without question. Suppose when we get back to Peshawar I make you orderly clerk in my office? You will be able then if you study, to enter the Indian Civil Service, for Lord Dalhousie, the Governor General, has replaced the old bad system of nomination from home by the Company's directors, by competitive examination. How does the idea appeal to you?"

"Why, thank you, sir, I'd love it!" cried Dicky, eyes sparkling with grateful excitement. "But—but can it be arranged, sir? The Colonel, sir——"

John Nicholson laughed softly.

"Oh, yes, it can be managed, never fear. You see, I'm a Brevet Colonel myself—my father, a Dublin physician, got me a commission in the Bengal Infantry, and I came to India in 1839 as ensign cadet, posted to the 27th Native Foot. I've only been an Administrative officer the last year or so!"

"Have you been in the Punjab long, sir?"

"Just four years. I acted as Deputy Commissioner at Bannu from 1851 until this spring—had plenty to do, too, settling the country after the Sikh wars. The Sikhs, you know, are a religious sect of warriors, founded by Yanaka Shah three hundred years ago. In 1764 they conquered the Punjab and they're bonny fighters who have given us a lot of trouble. When I first came here, though Lord Gough had beaten 'em soundly at Gujrat, they were still in open revolt, and fighting among themselves as well. But by God's help I managed to tame 'em down, and I think we understand each other pretty well now! I founded a force of Irregular Horse, to keep them amused, paying them very well, and they providing their own saddles and weapons."

"Are these hill men Sikhs, sir?" asked Dicky, deeply interested.

John Nicholson frowned, and he replied sternly, "No, they are wolves of Pathans, the Indian name for all those who live in Afghanistan and its borders. India is a strange, wonderful country, Marvel, peopled by races who have less in common between them than the nations of Europe. As you learnt to-day, wrestling with Dev Sahai, the Indian doesn't look at things as we do; he is clever, sensitive, and cunning; terribly ready to take offence, and become, by our standards, treacherous, if he suspects his religion or customs or honour have been slighted, even in a small way. Lord Dalhousie is one of the best Governors the Company, or India, ever had, but he did a very foolish thing when he insisted on sending the Bengal Infantry to fight in Persia. By leaving India, the Hindu sepoys lost caste. But there are, of course, many clever and honourable Hindus who are our loyal friends, and the Sikh, for example, is as fine and upright as any English gentleman. Up here in the hills, however, dwell tribes who cannot be trusted at all. 'Trust a mad dog before a snake, and a snake before a Pathan,' so runs the proverb!"

He stared with sombre eyes into the fire, and went on, "There will be no peace in the north till the Afghans are utterly crushed. They are sly, cunning, and envious; treacherous to the last degree, though our own statesmen aren't without blame, trying to impose weak kings on them! Only last year the Mahsud Wazirs raided the border, and killed Zeman Khan, one of my most valued native lieutenants!"

Dicky, rather puzzled by this reference to "weak kings," observed, "Dev Sahai and his uncle called them Pandis, sir!"

"Oh, that was just the family name of the tribe that attacked the fort. It's as common a name in India as Smith in England, though not so much up here, where the tribes are mostly Mussulmen, as in the Oudh and round Bombay. There are Pandis in the sepoy regiments whom I would trust with my life! But I wouldn't trust an Afghan Pandi any further than I could see him!"

"Is the present Afghan king a weak one, sir?" Dicky inquired.

"The Amir Dost Mahomed?" Nicholson chuckled. "Far from it. He's a stout old warrior, but he's also, I believe, sincerely anxious to see his country peacefully settled and to be friendly with us. The trouble is, Marvel, that to develop India we have had to break up some of the Northern states into smaller territories, so that they are less powerful. Kashmir, for example, was once part of the great Sikh empire, as was this border country. Ten years ago the Company tried to impose Shah Suja, a weak man, upon the Afghans, and there was a rebellion, a dreadful affair. I was in it, and captured for a while, and my brother Alexander was killed, ambushed when on patrol with two or three troopers. I discovered his poor naked mutilated body lying in the snow!" John Nicholson paused a moment, then went on, "General Elphinstone, in command at Kabul, was an old man, and lost his head completely. Down came Akbar Khan from the hills, and our fine army of fifteen thousand men was trapped and massacred in the Khurd Kabul Pass, only one man, Dr. Elphinston, escaping to tell the tale! An appalling disaster! Dost Mahomed had to be restored to his throne, and the Pathans now think all feringhees are fair game. However, we taught 'em a sharp lesson to-day. That story about the reign of the British Raj lasting for one hundred years gave us a chance to turn the tables on them beautifully. It's not the first time, I've heard it, though, and I can't say," he added half to himself, "I particularly care for the sound of it. There are ominous fires smouldering beneath the surface."

He stretched himself, and yawned, then turned to Dicky with a smile.

"It's time you were off to sleep, youngster. You've had a long day. Turn in now in those blankets the headman brought—I shook most of the fleas out of 'em!"

"Yes, sir," said Dicky, scrambling to his feet and saluting. "Er—wouldn't you like me to stay on guard, sir?"

"Thank you, Marvel," replied Nicholson, flexing his arms with another vast yawn, "but it won't be necessary. I'm a popular target, you know, but so far no one's had any luck. Quite recently a poor religious fanatic went for me with a sword—I grabbed a musket from a sentry and shot him through the chest[1]—and the natives now think a genie[2] guards me! No, we shall be quite safe. Good-night!"

Cantering through the fateful valley the next morning, John Nicholson paused to collect those bones and skulls whose rags of uniform and scraps of flesh showed them to have been white men,

[1] An actual incident—*Author*. [2] Demon—*Author*.

burying them beneath a pile of rocks and reading over them a few words from a prayer book he drew from the breast of his coat.   Then they rode on again to Peshawar, where John Nicholson led away the pony—Dicky was not sorry to see it go—while Dicky made his own way to the cantonments two miles outside the city walls.

Chapter Four

THE DEPUTY COMMISSIONER

THE EIGHTY-SEVENTH REGIMENT OF FOOT were out on manœuvres, but Dicky found a small guard left in a barracks near the main gates. Those men not on duty greeted him with ironical cheers as he entered.

"Holy Saint Pathrick! 'Tis Mister Marvel!" cried Private O'Brien, "and wivout his drum, bedad! Sorrow will be your portion when the rigiment returns, me bonny bhoy!"

Said Private Murphy, "Can I believe it? Sure and I thought the haythens had cut you up for chops days ago!"

"Not him," said Private Bell, rolling off his cot to pinch Dicky's arm painfully. "There's not enough on him to whet the appetite of an oyster!"

"It's a remarrkable thing my blessed eyes have seen," observed Private Barney solemnly, coming in off sentry go. "The Lootenant's been stabbed in the neck, poor old Colour Sergeant Sam Flint—the saints presarve him!—got shot where he can't sit down, meself has had the closest shave I iver want from a gint who ain't a barber, but our Dickybird goes prancing off, proud as a paycock, with the Deputy Commissioner. With my own eyes did I see it—the drhummer boy of the old Eighty-seventh Rigiment a-ridin' in bold as brass wiv Mister John Nicholson!"

Dropping his musket with a crash into its rack, he sat down, loosening his collar with a sigh of relief, and stared at Dicky with bewildered astonishment.

"By the same token he'll be invitin' us all up to the Residincy next, to dine off of ostrich eggs and elephants' tails, sarved up on gold plates by niggers wiv diamonds in their hats!"

"Would he have inny of the rajah's jools on him d'ye think?" observed Private Bell, turning to his companions.

"Sure, and we can see," cried Private O'Brien, seizing the luckless Dicky in an iron grip.

Despite his yells and protests, the grinning infantrymen up-ended him, and shook him like a giant rattle.

"Phwat's that?" cried Private Murphy after several breathless minutes.

"'Tis only a button!" said Private Bell sadly, and the infantrymen sat down on their cots and shook their heads.

"Bad cess to it!" said Private Barney suddenly. "He's hidden them in his boots!"

So they took Dick's boots off, then his trousers, and pulled his tunic over his back. But without result.

"There's only one answer to it, me bhoys," said Private Murphy, scratching his head, "he's swallowed 'em!"

"Sure, and I thought I heard a chinking when I

prodded him just now!" Private Bell jumped to his feet. "Poor young feller. I'll just step out and get a nice dose o' that black physic from the hospital orderly. Why, he might have the awful stomach ache!"

"Oh, please, Mister Barney," cried Dicky tearfully, "don't physic me again! I was awfully sick last time!"

"Why, that's right!" said Private Barney. "So you were—outrageous sick. Ah, well, we'll buy him some sherbet instead, eh, me lads? Straighten yoursilf out thin—ye're a disgrace to the Rigiment—and kim on down to the bazaar wiv us. An bring the Cherub wiv you, too!"

For Horace George Duff, the second regimental drummer boy, was also present, although he had gone to earth beneath the musketry rack when the fun began. Now he cautiously peered out with his round china-blue eyes, and dragged his slim form warily erect.

"I haven't reported I'm back yet," said Dicky, struggling with his boots, whilst Private Bell carelessly ruffled the "Cherubs" yellow curls.

"You'll have to report to that spalpane Sergeant O'Connell," replied Private Murphy, "and he'll not be back till ' Lights Out! '"

Giving their names at the gate to the corporal in charge, they strolled out on to the dusty road, and made for the city's crowded streets. Torches gleamed attractively on the goods for sale in the main bazaar

—beaten silver ware from Srinagar, copper vessels and ornaments from Benares, silks and gay shawls from Kashmir, weapons ornamented by the famous local craftsmen with gold and silver wire—but Private O'Brien said the crowds made him feel faint. And as Private Murphy had just had an argument with an Afghan horse-dealer, which had ended abruptly in the Afghan sitting down in the middle of a peddler's crockery, the crowd had grown rather noisy. So they elbowed their way out of the throng, and making their way to an open-air circus, sat down on the ground, quaffing sherbet, and buying sweets from the wandering vendors who cried their wares among the audience.

At the moment they entered, a snake charmer was wailing through a reed flute to several ugly reptiles writhing in a basket. After a few more minutes, however, Private O'Brien declared he was bored.

"'Tiz impossible!" cried Private Murphy. "Whoi, that beautiful music reminds me 'o the wake o' me poor old grandad! Whirrah, me feet are itchin' this minute!"

And, jumping up, he folded his arms, and began skipping in a wild jig round the snake charmer. Not to be outdone, Private Barney got up, laid a hand on Private Murphy's arm, and bowed to him solemnly. Then they began tripping in and out, clasping each other's horny hands, letting out wild shrieks, and snapping their fingers like a couple of madmen.

"Hurroo for ould Ireland!" screamed Private Bell,

jumping up to join them, but the infuriated audience began crowding round, chattering fiercely in their beards. A tall sepoy, a fine figure in his red coat and white trousers, stood up, and cried in perfect English:

"You feringhees would be wise to leave at once! We do not desire your company!"

"'Tis insultin' me poor old grandad he is!" spluttered Private Murphy. "Let me at the black haythen!"

"Sure, and is this a private fight, Mister Murphy? Or can innyone join in?" shouted Private Barney, doubling his fists.

"Stop it, ye fools," said Private O'Brien in a low voice. "Rimimber what the Colonel said about startin' a riot!"

So they pushed out of the menacing crowd, Private O'Brien towing after him by the coat-tails Private Murphy, who was brandishing his fists and inviting all and sundry "jist to step up and have a basinful"—an invitation which to his bitter regret was not accepted.

"May I be moidered and fried in oil if I know what's come over the sepoys recently," mused Private Bell as they made their way home.

"Sure, they think they're as good as us—and better—all of a sudden," agreed Private Murphy with a longing look back. "Whoi did ye not let me clout yon black-faced omadhaun, for the honour of the rigiment and the glory of ould Ireland?"

"In the hills an Afghan said the reign of the British Raj would only last a hundred years," piped up Dicky, "but Mr. Nicholson pointed out that the prophecy began in 1757, and this is the year 1856! So they gave him the man who attacked the fort, and Mr. Nicholson made them hang him!"

There was a roar of appreciative laughter from the infantrymen.

"Ah, 'tis a broth of a bhoy he is, the great John Nicholson!" cried Private Murphy admiringly.

At that moment John Nicholson was sitting in his shirt sleeves at a table crowded with papers. Despite his exertions of the last few days he had paused only for a good wash and some food before plunging into the mass of office routine awaiting him. By his elbow sat a native clerk, who, from time to time, made notes at his direction on a memorandum slip, and opposite him the Resident Commissioner, Mr. Herbert Edwardes, a quiet mannered man with a stern mouth, with whom he discussed various problems that arose.

Midnight had struck before they retired, but at five o'clock John Nicholson was up and about again, and after breakfast rode out of the city gates to meet Brigadier-General Neville Chamberlain, Commandant of the Punjab Irregular Horse, who were engaged on manœuvres with the 87th Foot.

With him went two ensign cadets from the East India Company's military college at Addiscombe, in Surrey; fresh-faced young Englishmen only recently arrived in India, and who were to see a little of the native forces before being posted to their regiments.

Nicholson led them south-west into a spur of the foot-hills, the cadets chattering excitedly, gazing round them open-eyed at the caravans that passed, odorous with teas and spices, the beggars squatting with their wooden begging bowls in the dust, the mendicant priests, the tiny temples hung with votive offerings of scraps of cloth and metal, the watchmen nursing old flint-lock muskets in the towers overlooking the stony fields where bare-footed women hoed their scanty crops. With the exception of the priests, who crouched and bared their teeth in a mirthless grin, everyone who saw Nicholson threw themselves flat on the ground, or salaamed deeply, throwing dust on their heads. In the villages they were greeted by loud shouts, the potter leaving his wheel, the shepherd his flock, to run after Nicholson, beseeching his blessing—actions which made the cadets open their astonished eyes even wider.

Once they were met by a little procession of horsemen, all armed to the teeth, escorting a palanquin whose curtains were of blue silk embroidered with scarlet flowers and gold thread.

At sight of Nicholson, the escort whipped out their swords in salute; the leader, a fine swashbuckling ruffian in a green turban, lifting his right arm high over his head and shouting, "All hail, mighty one! Good fortune attend thee!"

"God be with thee, O Chand Aggarwala," replied Nicholson, reining in his horse and returning the salute. "Do you ride in these hills with only twenty troopers to guard the lily?"—indicating the palanquin.

"Ah, bah," roared the ruffian. "Since thou dwellest among us, Nikkal Seyn, all is peace, and a man cannot find excuse even for a small bickering. In this land, once so happy and warlike, a maid can now walk unharmed from end to end of the province, and my escort are but to honour the Princess Nana el Dum, who journeys to wed my father, Amin Ahmad!"

"May they both live in happiness a thousand years," said Nicholson, and rode on.

As the ensigns clattered after him, the curtains of the palanquin moved, a slender dusky hand appeared, and two bright eyes shone from within.

"Don't look at her!" warned Nicholson sharply. His own eyes were fixed on the road ahead. "If she is seen by a white man, she will be strangled, not wed, in the palace to-night! Remember that, you two, a high born Indian lady must never be seen unveiled, or her life will pay the price for your carelessness!"

They found the 87th Foot skirmishing in open order among the rocks in a little valley, hotly attacked by the Punjab Horse, who charged down on them from time to time with wild yells, leaping their horses fearlessly over every obstacle, right into the bayonets and banging blank cartridges at the exasperated Irishmen.

Brigadier Chamberlain rode among them, shouting hoarse orders, directing and encouraging, smiling in his beard as the cursing infantrymen dodged hurriedly out of the way of the horsemen, who with their eleven-foot lances strapped across their backs, swept down on them, swords dancing wickedly in the sun.

At the head of the valley the Colonel of the 87th Foot sat gloomily on his horse, accompanied by one or two of his officers, and Nicholson galloped up to him.

"My troop seem to be doing well," he remarked after greetings had been exchanged and the two cadets introduced.

The Colonel, yellow faced and elderly, with a long, white, drooping moustache, was a ripe specimen of the conventional army pattern—stupid, honourable, and entirely ignorant of, and indifferent to, everything that lay outside army routine and regulations.

He turned a small dull eye on Nicholson, remarking, "Ridic'lus to expect infantry in open order to repel cavalry! Good for the men, no doubt, gives 'em a bit of exercise, but it's not war, you know, Mr. Nicholson, by Gad no! All this ridin' all over the place, what? Circus tricks, I call it! Can't win a battle with those games, dammit!"

"Still," said Nicholson with a twinkle, "you will admit the Punjab Horse have rapped the Pathans'

E

knuckles pretty smartly on more than one occasion recently?"

"Chasing a lot of hairy lunatics? What? But supposin' the beggars had formed square and met you with regular volleys? Eh? That's what wins an action, Mr. Nicholson. H-r-rumph! Regular volley firin'—I remember my grandad tellin' me how a few volleys from the British squares at Waterloo blew the French cuirassiers into powder—into powder, by Gad, sir!"

Brigadier Chamberlain spurred up, white with dust, and leant from his saddle to clasp Nicholson's hand warmly.

"By Jove, Nicholson, these Sikhs of yours are a fine lot!" he cried enthusiastically. "Some of the best material I've ever handled!"

"The Colonel calls them a circus," replied Nicholson drily.

The Brigadier frowned, and an edge came into his voice.

"We're not on a parade ground, Colonel. Any regiment might be caught in open or skirmishing order by cavalry, even our own splendid infantrymen, whom the world has cause to know are second to none. And the Punjab Horse must be exercised. One day we may be very glad of them indeed, especially if any serious trouble started, which Heaven forbid!"

John Nicholson nodded.

"Amen to that wish," he remarked gravely.

"Russia would be delighted to take her revenge by embarrassing us in India while so many of our forces are still in the Crimea. Undoubtedly she instigated that trouble in Persia, and I've a shrewd suspicion that Russian-paid agitators are making trouble now, all over the province!"

"The Crimean War, I'm afraid, was ill-advised," said the Brigadier. "We had no real quarrel with Russia, and our old allies should be our friend, not enemy!"

The Colonel stirred impatiently.

"A stiff volley would have settled the business one way or the other immediately," he grumbled. "Well, gentlemen, time for tiffin, I think!"

As bugles shrilled in the valley, and they sat down to a rough meal, Nicholson remarked:

"I want to take one of your drummer boys, Colonel!"

"One of my drummer boys?" repeated the elderly warrior in amazement. "What the dooce for? Beastly little brats—no sense of discipline, h-rump."

"His name is Richard Marvel," said Nicholson. "I want to make him a clerk in my office!"

The Colonel would dearly like to have refused, but he could not think of a reasonable excuse. Moreover, the Brigadier was watching him, and he knew that Nicholson was not only a personal friend of Major-General Reade, the Military Commanding Officer at Peshawar—as he was indeed of all the district officials, military and civilian—but also thought very highly of by those whom the Colonel called "The Powers that Be."

Therefore he blew out his moustache, scowled, and with a very ill-grace gave in.

"Only hope it won't unsettle the men, what? Give 'em ideas, if you see what I mean? Pickin' out brats from the ranks—h-r-rrumph!"

Chapter Five

A DUEL WITH BHANDARI

ONE MORNING a month later Dicky nervously entered the cool hall of the Civilian Administration Offices. Two or three Babu clerks glanced at him curiously, and one approached, and after courteously inquiring his business, asked him to wait a moment.

Dicky sat down on a stool, staring round him, and wondering what new experiences lay ahead. The previous night he and the Cherub had had a farewell supper together in a native canteen favoured by white soldiers. There they were discovered by Privates Murphy and O'Brien, who sat down un-invited beside them.

"Phwat horrible sight is this?" demanded Private Murphy, severely. "Is it not a disgrace the way the young gorge themselves these days, Mister O'Brien?"

"It is that," agreed the infantryman, stretching out his hand to some fruit. "Weally wevoltin', as Ensign Neill would say! Phwat is that in that wooden bowl? Pigs' trotters?"

"Poisoning their little stummicks," said Private Murphy. "Holy Saint Patrick, this stuff in the blue jar tastes like tar and boot blacking! Now, whatever good would a man get from sich stuff? Give me a nice bit of haddick seethed in milk and praise be, I'll foight the whole rigiment. But do you suppose, Mister O'Brien, these poor haythens have iver hearrd of a haddick?"

71

Private O'Brien, cautiously inspecting the contents of a green bottle, shook his head vigorously.

"'Tis a quare country, India," he observed. "Down here 'tis as hot as the gates of hell, but a few miles away, in them outrageous mountains, ye have to look sharp y're dinner doesn't freeze before ye can ate it!"

"Sure 'tis a quare country," replied Murphy. "Here's meself been serrvin' the Queen—God bless her—wiv sich bhoys as yoursilf for yearrs and yearrs, wivout so much as one invitation from the Governor. Faith, I wonder sometimes whether he knows we're here at all! Yet little Dicky gets took up by the Commissioner, and goes off, proud as a camil wiv three humps, to sit drinkin' chota pegs while beautiful houris polish his boots! It is a shame, it is, for the rigiment will miss you, Mister Marvel!"

"The curse of Crummle on thim that denies it!" growled Private O'Brien who was growing rather truculent on the contents of the green bottle.

There was a rough affection behind their words which quite touched Dicky and he asked permission —readily granted—to buy them drinks, in which they drank his very good health, and good luck.

Fortunately the Colonel had been so indignant at having Dicky thrust upon his notice that he quite forgot to ask about the drum, and Dicky was wondering idly where it had got to, when the clerk returned and ushered him into Mr. Edwardes' office.

"So you are Richard Marvel, eh?" said Mr. Edwardes, shaking his hand and giving him a keen look. "You'll find your new life very like your old one, for we are all under semi-military discipline, even in this office. I am attaching you to Mr. Nicholson, at his request, but for the time being you won't have any definite duties, except to make yourself generally useful, particularly to Mr. Nicholson. We must see how you shape before giving you a definite post. This morning you can assist Fazir," he indicated a clerk in the corner, "to copy entries into those ledgers. I do want you to realise your future is now in your own hands. Learn the native dialects, study the history of the Company, gain all the knowledge you possibly can about native customs and ways of life. India, Marvel, is a strange, vast country, which offers splendid opportunities for a full and valuable life to men who are keen, and brave, and thorough!"

Over an hour passed, and then the door opened, and Nicholson himself appeared, dressed in spotless white drill, and with a portfolio under his arm. Nodding with an amused smile at Dicky, he sat down at Mr. Edwardes' table. The two men talked in low tones for a moment, then Mr. Edwardes raised his eyebrows, nodded, and glanced across at Dicky, absorbed in his ledger. Rising, he consulted a huge map hanging on the wall, and sat down again, bending his head over some papers he drew from the portfolio. The two men conferred together in lowered voices, more than once rising to stare at the map, while Dicky, his fingers finding a pen strange after the drum sticks, painfully but doggedly continued to make entries, his round sprawling hand in startling relief against the clerk's small neat characters. From time to time he caught scraps of the hushed conversation across the room.

"Our forces, of course, are divided into the three Divisions of Bombay, Madras, and Bengal," said Mr. Edwardes, staring at the map. "The Bombay Division at the moment holds the largest number of white troops!"

John Nicholson made a quiet rejoinder, and the Commissioner nodded.

"Yes, the largest number of sepoys are quartered in the Bengal section where the Bengal Infantry, for example, are mostly drawn from the Hindus of the Oudh and Ganges. Our sepoy cavalry are mostly Mahomedans, and I think fairly trustworthy. What we lack most are white officers of the right type These Russian wars have drained all our best away!"

He glanced over the papers in his hand.

"Major-General Reade and Brigadier Sidney Cotton must see these," he remarked. "Sir John Lawrence (he meant the High Commissioner) will be very interested, too!"

His voice sank again, and there were several more minutes of earnest conversation, then John Nicholson observed:

"My spies report there is a great outcry about the

new locomotives. The Hindus, particularly the Brahmin priests, were frightened of the telegraph, and some now say this new monster will devour them all!"

Mr Edwardes laughed heartily.

"A revolution caused by a steam-engine will be something new in history! However, let's hope our fears don't materialise, although I agree there are ugly rumours flying about!"

John Nicholson rose, and shook the Commissioner's hand.

"Keep Gulab Singh in a good humour," said Mr. Edwardes. "It will be a tragedy if he's upset! Good luck!"

With a nod of the head, John Nicholson left the table, and crossed over to Dicky, leaning over the back of his chair.

"Well, Marvel, got your foot on the first rung of the ladder, eh? Get those entries finished, and then this afternoon go to the barracks and ask for Harbans Singh Bhandari, a native sergeant-instructor of the Punjab Horse. Mr. Edwardes has agreed to let you off for the next few days to gain a little experience in horsemanship. Bhandari is expecting you, and learn all you possibly can from him, not only how to ride, but something about horses—how they are shod, and how to feed and water and groom them. In a few days I'm going off on a routine circuit of inspection, and I expect you would like to be my orderly!"

So Dicky duly presented himself at the barracks, and found Harbans Bhandari to be a bow-legged, thick-set sinister looking Sikh with a beard curled under his chin, and one nostril considerably enlarged by an old sword-cut wound.

The Indian stared searchingly into his eyes, and then remarked:

"I think you have met Zafar Sahai and his nephew? Some small matter of a drum, was there not?"

"Oh, do you know Dev?" cried Dicky.

"I am related to his family by marriage, my wife being a cousin of Yusuf Khan! But to business!"

He walked slowly round and round Dicky, inspecting him like a horse.

"Your legs are long and muscular," he observed at last. "Your body thin, so that they do not have to carry any weight, and your arms also are long and thin. Good. I think I can make something of you. Were there time, I might make a swordsman of you also. As you will learn, long legs are useful to grip the horse's ribs, whilst your body is not of a weight to topple you out of the saddle. To be a horseman, or a swordsman, or both, you understand, a man should be either short and muscular, or tall, lean, and long limbed. Your short man is compact, powerful, all his weight and energy packed into a small space; whilst the tall lean man has as a rule a narrow body, easily supported by his legs, which, because of his height, Nature has made sinewy and tough. Moreover, his long arms give him a wide reach. Where the short man hacks and slashes, face to face with the foe, the tall one stands apart, his sword protecting him in a circle of steel as he twirls his wrist—and thus he avoids such accidents as this!" and Bhandari tapped his scarred nose with a twisted smile. "How old are you, young feringhee?"

"Fourteen," said Dicky.

"Good," said Bhandari again. "Though to be a perfect horseman one should begin lessons in childhood, you are supple yet, and your bones will not be set. Now, Mahmadoollah!" he cried to a groom. "Is the blind pony saddled and waiting?"

When, on the evening of the fourth day, John Nicholson rode on to the barrack square, Dicky, though far from being a perfect rider, at least felt very much more at home in the saddle than when he last rode.

He had learnt how to sit straight, the ball of his foot on the stirrup iron, how to rise on that iron when his mount began to trot, how to clamp in his knees and sit back when it broke into a canter. Hour after hour he had ridden round the sawdust bed on which the troopers exercised, learning, too, how to swing his body from the hips when there were jumps ahead. Afterwards he had accompanied the grooms back to the stalls, and helped bed the horses down, growing to know the use of dandy-brush and curry-comb, and one morning he had spent in the forge, watching how the farriers prepared the horses' hooves and shod them. The following morning he had returned to the forge, for it was the day when Mr. Frank Maker, a civilian veterinary surgeon, rode over to lecture on first aid to horses to the native non-commissioned officers and any others who were interested. Naturally enough, he usually had a big audience of absorbed natives of all ranks, for on the welfare of their charges depended the life of the cavalrymen. Dicky was interested to learn that Mr. Maker, a dapper little man from Kent, with a bald head and bony sensitive fingers that quivered like an insect's antennæ, had trained and taken his diploma at the Royal Veterinary College in London. Dicky had once seen the College, standing amid the fields of Kentish Town, on a trip to Hampstead. He watched intently as the surgeon bent to run searching fingers over the left hind cannon of the injured horse standing in the centre of the circle, explaining to his audience the difference between sprains and bony growths as a cause of lameness; and thought to himself what a lot Mr. Maker must know, and how useful he was, for he also attended the hump-backed native cattle, camels, dogs, and even elephants, with equal success.

As John Nicholson dismounted, and strode over to them, Bhandari sprang smartly to attention, and Dicky, who was strapping up the girths of his mount, followed his example.

"What progress has your pupil made, O Harbans Bhandari?" inquired Nicholson, returning the salute.

"He has still much to learn, lord, but his heart is

stout, and with practice he should soon become adept!"

"Excellent," said Nicholson. "Of course he has been fortunate in his instructor." A compliment at which Bhandari flushed with pleasure. "To-morrow morning, Marvel, we ride out at dawn. Will you be ready?"

"Yes, sir," replied Dicky, saluting.

"Very well. Come to my quarters, where a horse will be ready for you."

"Do you wish for a little exercise before you depart, lord?" said Bhandari eagerly.

John Nicholson looked at him, and a slow smile spread over his mobile features.

"O, thou wicked old wolf!" he said. "Cunning as the mongoose, dost wish to avenge thy last defeat? Come then, bring shields and the practice swords!"

And he unwound his sash and carefully peeled off his coat, whilst the Sikh, grinning with delight, shouted a string of orders, and then led the way to the gymnasium—a long building with open arches in the walls.

Dick handed over his horse to a groom and followed after, Bhandari whispering, "Now shalt thou see a fight to remember always! Remember my words as to that which makes a swordsman!"

Word had already flown round the barracks, and from every quarter bearded troopers came running, crowding in at the arched colonnades to watch with bated breath the sham duel now in progress.

The Indian fashion of sword-fighting is to carry
a small round embossed shield, and leap to and fro,
cutting savagely with a light curved sabre or
tulwar. Dicky had seen performers before in the
circuses, and the duellists' swift leaps to and fro
always reminded him of a pair of game-cocks.
Nicholson often carried the heavy straight European
sword of a dragoon, but on this occasion he fought
Bhandari native fashion.

But he was too big a man to crouch and leap from
side to side.

Swaying lithely from the waist, he used his length
of arm both to extend his shield and to deliver
vicious sweeps that time and time again Bhandari
escaped only by jumping high into the air. Sparks
flew from the shields, the tulwars clashed and
rang like silversmiths' hammers, and the watching
Sikhs shouted and screamed encouragement and
admiration.

At last Bhandari grew desperate, and creeping up
on his adversary, suddenly extended his left arm
high above his head, under Nicholson's sword arm,
at the same time slashing savagely at his body. But
Nicholson only laughed, chopped downward with
his sword hilt, almost breaking the Sikh's wrist,
caught the swing on his shield, and continuing his
downward stroke, swept the pugaree[1] almost
completely off the Sikh's head. Then he laughed
again, and throwing aside shield and sword, caught

[1] Light turban—*Author.*

Bhandari's left arm, pulled him towards him, caught his right arm, and bent to swing him over his shoulder. A gasp of amazement went up from the audience as Bhandari, immensely powerful, struggled fiercely but in vain to break the iron grip on his arms. Grinning and snarling with rage, he dropped his own sword and shield, and strove to grapple Nicholson to him in his turn, his burly body writhing and twisting, the great muscles standing out like knotted ropes. There was a tense pause. Bhandari's reputation, not only as swordsman, but as wrestler, was now at stake. He tried every trick known to him, but he might as well have tried to tear a boulder from its bed. Dicky saw Nicholson's great shoulders ripple and set as he met the onslaught, then a sudden gasp burst from the Sikh; for one second he lost his balance, and in that instant John Nicholson plucked him clear off his feet, held him for one long sinew-cracking moment over his head, then gently put him down again, and with a breathless chuckle shook his head and patted him admiringly on the back.

A deep-throated murmur of awe and wonder ran round the audience.

"O, Lal Chanda," cried one tall Sikh, "pay me thy two rupees, for thou hast lost thy bet! Surely Nikkal Seyn is indeed the God of War, come from Heaven to dwell among us!"

And there was a unanimous chorus of agreement from his comrades.

Chapter Six

THE JUDGMENT OF
NIKKAL SEYN

DURING the days that followed, Dicky rode after John Nicholson east across the Punjab into Kashmir, and then south to Srinagar.

They travelled slowly, for on each afternoon a halt was made at a village where Nicholson sat down with the headman to advise on questions of agriculture and taxes, and sometimes to give judgment on other matters.

Agriculture was always the greatest problem, for the ryots, or Hindu cultivators, were mostly very poor, and their herds of cattle miserable thin beasts who could get little food from the barren fields. Ploughs and hoes were of primitive pattern, and since cow-dung was commonly used for fuel—wood being valuable—there was very little manure to improve fertility of the soil. The peasant indeed lived a life very near the border-line of starvation, and was utterly dependent upon the weather for his scanty handfuls of corn and barley and oats. Diseases such as rinderpest and red-water took heavy toll of his livestock, matters not being improved by the fact that since the cow is sacred to the Hindu, an animal was never allowed to be destroyed, however sick or near to death it might be. John Nicholson told Dicky about the semi-religious "pinjrapoles" and "gaushalas," homes of rest for derelict animals established in most of the cities throughout India, but which were of very little use, because the sick beasts, particularly the she-buffaloes, and cows and bullocks were seldom allowed to be given medical treatment of any kind by the white man. Each year, moreover, cattle-dealers drove tens of thousands of cattle from the frontier provinces and the Punjab, where they were bred and reared, down into the southern states, eating up the crops, and carrying with them many diseases they picked up from sickly beasts in the villages and the pinjrapoles and gaushalas.

"It's an enormous problem," he sighed, as Dicky wrote up notes he dictated for Mr. Edwardes' later perusal; "one that is becoming far too vast for a private company to tackle. Sooner or later the Crown must step in and help us to organise a complete medical, educational, and veterinary service. Fancy, Marvel, in 1814 the East India Company owned little more than the district round Calcutta, and now, only forty years later, we have the whole of India to administer. The old idea of fighting for concessions to trade has quite been swamped. God, or Fate, has thrust an enormous task on us, as Lord Dalhousie has realised. We must help the peoples of India all we can, particularly the great mass of illiterate peasants, who have been down-trodden and crushed for centuries, even though at first they don't appreciate our efforts. The rajahs and petty squires are, many of them, suspicious of us, too, but they will recognise in time that we feringhees are not just one more wave of conquerors, thirsty for loot and power. We have come to break the chains of slaves, to raise the fallen, to bind up the wounds of the injured. And that is what we are going to do, even though, being only men ourselves, we may make mistakes and commit some silly blunders!"

Each village had its own particular troubles: apart from the endless discussions on crops and live-stock, a lion (of which more later) had carried off a peasant's wife, a witch had put a curse on a blind man's goat, cholera or fever had broken out, or there was some domestic tangle requiring consider-able thought and care to unravel.

An elderly Hindu came, seeking assistance, for his wife had run away with a handsome young man. The aggrieved husband had therefore demanded the return of his dowry from the girl's father, who refused to pay it.

"Let the wife, and the young man, and the girl's father, stand before me," said Nicholson.

The village guards returned, accompanied by a thick-set Hindu with a grey beard, and a tall youth whose expression was dogged and sullen, his right arm thrown protectively round a dusky beauty whose eyes flashed furiously above her veil. As the guards stood back, she jerked herself angrily away from her lover, stepping forward to pour out a flood of shrill abuse at Nicholson.

He made no sign, however, but sat regarding her calmly, and her voice died away, and then stopped abruptly under his steady gaze.

Minutes passed whilst Nicholson sat motionless, considering the trio, who fidgeted uneasily, the villagers glancing from them to the massive figure in the white drill, nudging and whispering to each other.

"Who knows this girl?" inquired Nicholson at length.

A nervous village woman was thrust forward. "I am her aunt, lord!"

"Has she always spoken in such an angry voice?"

"She is an only child, lord, and without a mother's care has, perhaps, known too much freedom. Her father could do nothing with her, and at me, her aunt, she has more than once thrown a stew-pot!"

Nicholson waved her aside and leant forward.

"This is my judgment. The young man has done evil in taking the woman from her husband's house. Therefore, let her who tempted him beat him with thirty whippings. And since her father, and her husband, could not rule their own households in peace, let her father return to the husband the dowry he was given, for the woman is worth nothing till she has learnt humility. But as the husband is well rid of her, let him pay to that young man the dowry he gave the girl's father, thus salving the young man's bruises!"

Women are not regarded in India as they are in

England, and Nicholson knew well that nothing would so humiliate the girl as having to whip her lover. And indeed his sentence pleased every one, except perhaps the father and the husband, who stared at each other in dismay; and the young man, who turned to shake a furious fist at Nicholson as he was dragged away with the screaming girl.

Dicky was sitting, engrossed in the scene, a few paces behind the Deputy Commissioner, and out of the corner of his eye saw the figure of a one-eyed fakir, dressed in trailing, ragged robes, step from the trees that bordered the lane behind. As the fakir's solitary eye fell upon the mighty figure of John Nicholson, however, he dodged back again into cover. There was something so queer and furtive in his action that Dicky was about to call Nicholson's attention, only at that moment the Deputy Commissioner rose and turned to him.

"Office work, Marvel," he said with a genial smile. "Come along, and let's get my reports entered up! You know, Marvel," he said as they walked back to the house where they were lodging, "I met you, as our French allies would say, *a la bonne heure*! Just at the right time. I've often wanted to have a clerk with me, but poor old Fazir is too fat to go jogging about in the sun. And he's the only one of our native clerks I have ever really trusted. We've posted up recently some very confidential matters that I wouldn't care the Hindus to know about!"

"You mean all these rumours about a rebellion, sir?"

John Nicholson nodded.

"The Indian has experienced so many invasions he doesn't realise we white folk are totally different from the Moslems and Pathans who, at different times, have swept over his country. We have come to stay, but I hope a war won't be necessary to make them realise it!"

Early the next morning Dicky was saddling Nicholson's horse, whilst the Deputy Commissioner sat drinking a final cup of coffee. Dicky had noticed that John Nicholson never hurried except when there was need for haste; when resting, he relaxed completely, and was therefore always fresh and ready for action.

He glanced up with an inquiring look as the village headman approached with many low bows, observing:

"May we request your lordship's company to-day?"

"Why?" asked Nicholson. "I must ride on to the next village!"

"Please to stay with us, lord," the headman implored. "The—er—the roads are dangerous!"

"Come now, Rattan Garewal," said Nicholson. "Speak the truth! What is behind thy words?"

"Lord," wailed the headman, rubbing his hands nervously together, "the youth ye sentenced to be whipped has bribed two robbers to kill thee! Even now they lie in wait along the road!"

"Oh, is that all?" retorted Nicholson, coolly drinking off his coffee. "I thank thee, Garewal. Nikkal Seyn shall not forget thy kindness. And as for the youth, I trust your girl laid on shrewdly?"

"Indeed, yes, lord. His groans kept the village awake all night until cock-crow!"

"Good," said Nicholson. "Have the guards bring him here within the hour! Marvel, is my horse ready?"

"Yes, sir," said Dicky saluting.

Nicholson sprang into the saddle, and drew out the long cavalry sabre strapped to the saddle. Examining it carefully, he swung it round his head once or twice, and then trotted off down the village street.

"Shall I come, sir?" cried Dicky.

John Nicholson turned and smiled, but shook his head.

"Get everything packed, ready to move on at once!"

"He will be killed," whispered the headman fearfully. "Those who await him are master swordsmen who have long terrified travellers!"

Dicky could only understand a word or two of what he said, but he shook his head stoutly.

"Not our John Nicholson," he said sturdily, but hoped to himself he was right. A shot from an ambush would kill as effectively, and more safely, as a fight with cold steel.

The Deputy Commissioner rode on alone, until a few miles along the highway he saw before him a clump of rocks towering across the road. There was no one in sight at the moment, but as he set his horse to a gallop, two wild figures rode out from the rocks and reined in to meet him. Nicholson never paused, but urging his horse to greater speed, rode straight at the two assassins, who were brandishing swords and screaming insults. Too excited to wait, the foremost set off at a canter to meet him, stones and dust flying behind his pony's heels. With a crash Nicholson rode him down, and as he sprawled helpless, split his head from turban to chin with one terrific down-stroke. The second horseman leant from his saddle, and his tulwar bit the air with a harsh scream as Nicholson recovered and jerked his arm upward with his sabre hilt. For a moment they hacked and stabbed at each other, sparks flying in showers from the grinding blades, then Nicholson lunged with all the force of his arm.

A hideous bubbling yell echoed from the crags as the long sabre took the robber in the centre of his tangled beard and transfixed his throat from back to front. Nicholson disengaged his weapon, watched as the native toppled slowly from the saddle, blood pouring from his mouth, and then rode back to the village.[1]

"Clean this, Marvel," he said, handing Dicky his sword, "and get me another cup of coffee." To the headman, who was fluttering, open-eyed, around, he said, "On the high road not far away you will find

[1] An actual incident in Nicholson's life—*Author*.

the bodies of the two robbers. Bring them in, and let the young man who bribed them to kill me watch over them this day before they are thrown to the vultures. This will teach him not to dispute the judgment of Nikkal Seyn!"

Chapter Seven

LION-HUNT

THE affair of the lion proved quite a big business: a full-dress ceremonial which led to a visit to the palace of the local Rajah, Prince Seth Premchand of Mangrulkar. Lions were not common in the district, but sometimes came down from the hills, as this one had probably done. By the headman who informed Nicholson of its presence sat an equerry of the Rajah, who bore an invitation from the Prince to hunt the lion from his estate.

So the Deputy Commissioner had Dicky polish up his equipment till it shone, while Dicky himself brushed his coat and plastered his hair down so that it did not stick up at the back so much as usual, and then rode off after Nicholson and the equerry.

Emerging from some mango trees, they entered a grassy plain, beyond which rose the Rajah's palace, surrounded by extensive gardens ablaze with flowers and rhododendron bushes in full bloom. The air was heavy with their scent, and they splashed across a shallow stream, winding towards the palace, where huge ornamental carp scattered wildly under the horses' hooves—the biggest goldfish Dicky had ever seen.

After cantering for about a mile, they heard a native band in full and raucous blast, then about a score of swarthy guards armed to the teeth appeared, headed by trumpeters and drummers, and escorting three elephants with howdahs, or little cars, strapped to their backs. In the centre howdah, under a huge crimson umbrella with a gold fringe, sat the Prince, a lithe clean-shaven Hindu wearing a white drill suit, and with an enormous ruby set in his turban. The howdah behind him was empty, but the third carried the Prince's Master of Horse and one or two other officials. Grooms, leading a dozen horses, whose coats shone like silk brought up the rear, together with a mob of servants.

As Nicholson appeared, the elephant carrying the Prince was halted by its driver, and made to bend down on its knees. The Prince stood up and raised his arm in response to the Deputy Commissioner's salute, while Nicholson himself dismounted, and, approaching the Prince, touched his lips and his breast, and bowed slightly from the waist.

When greetings had been exchanged, the Prince observed that the best time to hunt lions was at dawn.

"To-morrow morning, however, I must bless the peasants' fields with holy water from the Ganges! So perhaps we may find sport this afternoon. There are reports that the lion has its lair in a nullah about three miles from here, and already my men lie hidden about its lip. If thou and I ride down into the valley, while they shout from above, we may rouse it from its noonday sleep!"

John Nicholson nodded.

"Your suggestions promise good sport. Shall thou and I ride alone?"

The Hindu smiled sadly, and threw out his hands despairingly.

"Alas, custom forbids it! My equerry at least must be with me. Hast thou a companion?"

The Deputy Commissioner smiled, and turned to indicate Dicky, whose mouth fell open.

"My orderly will attend me!"

"But he is but a youth—a skinny one at that!"

"Nevertheless he has fought in battle," said Nicholson. "He can carry a spare musket for me and load it as required!"

"As you will," answered the Hindu. "Doth thy slave's mouth always gape like a carp's?" he added. "Perchance it is a good thing—he will swallow the lion! Ha-ha!"

He beckoned his servants, and Dicky shut his mouth with a gulp as John Nicholson turned and frowned at him. He suspected what was in the wind, and asked with another gulp:

"Do I—am I to come with you, sir?"

"Yes, Marvel," said Nicholson crisply, running his eye over a musket handed to him. "You are to walk behind me to reload! Here are powder and ball!"

The nullah was about a mile long and a quarter of a mile broad, a deep cleft in the stony ground, in winter filled by a roaring torrent, but now sun-baked and empty. Half-way along its length a clump of withered bushes hung to the cliff face, casting into deep shade the tumbled boulders below. At this point lay a huge fallen tree, whose bark was ripped and peeled in many places. Another tree still stood near the opposing bank, its roots exposed by the winter torrents.

The Prince reined in his white Arab stallion at the mouth of the ravine and peered into its deep shadows.

"Beneath yonder fallen tree 'tis said the lion couches," he observed to Nicholson. "And from those bones in the water-bed, and those scratches where the beast has sharpened his claws, it would seem the truth!"

He stared down again into the nullah.

"A horse cannot descend either end nor those sheer slopes. We must go on foot! Bid the beaters wake the beast!"

A trumpet shrilled, drums thundered, invisible natives, posted along the sides of the nullah, set up a wild screaming and halloo-ing. With fierce answering shouts the Prince's guards galloped off among the rocks at either edge, waving their swords and firing their muskets into the air, till the noise reached pandemonium.

Suddenly from the rocks beneath the shrubs came a deep menacing growl.

Instantly the noise ceased, only to break out into renewed clamour as a shadow moved and a sinister tawny form crept out into the sunlight, baring white teeth in furious snarls at its enemies above, which the lion could scent but not see.

The Prince promptly slipped agilely from his saddle. When he was on the ground, Nicholson followed suit, and Dicky more slowly copied his example. Musket in hand, the Rajah and the Deputy Commissioner walked towards where the ground tumbled down into the valley, the equerry and Dicky following them, each with a spare musket over his shoulder.

As the Rajah took the first descending step, a wild figure burst from the watchful crowd of servants behind.

"Back, O Prince Premchand of Mangrulkar! Go not down into the valley, for it is death!" A shaking hand was thrust against the Rajah's breast. "The lion killed a girl, 'tis true, but 'twas at Shiva's behest. To shoot the lion is to anger Shiva!"

A tall Brahmin, a priest of the Prince's household, strode forward.

"Be warned in time, my lord, lest Shiva cast thy soul into the uttermost pit, where devils will torment thee for three thousand years!"

Powerful as are the princes of India, they are helpless before the priests of their religion. The Rajah hesitated, glanced down into the nullah, where the lion, ripping the air with vicious claws, was now only about five hundred yards away, frowned, bit his lip, and backed slowly on to the high ground.

"Forgive me, Nikkal Seyn," he said in unexpectedly fluent English, and glanced at the Brahmin in his greasy robes of pink and yellow, the Hindu colours, and the newcomer, a long-haired, one-eyed fakir in a tattered gown.

Nicholson himself hesitated. Though an unbeliever, expected to have no respect for the hundred odd gods of Hindu mythology, he did not wish to embarrass the Prince by doing anything out of place.

But at this moment Dicky thrust forward excitedly, for he had recognised the newcomer.

"Sir—that priest—I've seen him before——"

The fakir, stroking his beard and craftily smiling to himself, was standing very near the edge of the nullah. As Dick pointed at him, he started violently, turned to run, slipped on loose pebbles, and fell down into the nullah with a terrified yell which was answered by a savage roar from the lion.

"That settles it," said Nicholson. "Gods or no gods, I can't see that crazy idiot torn in pieces! Come on, Marvel!"

Prince Premchand took a step forward, but the Brahmin, not anxious to see a possible rival rescued, laid one hand solemnly on his breast, pointing with the other to the sky and shaking his head.

Down into the nullah climbed Nicholson, Dicky scrambling after, while the lion bounded forward with blood-curdling growls, and the fakir, scrambling to his feet, screamed, and screamed again until the valley rang.

"Good lad," said Nicholson as he and Dicky reached the boulders below. "Is that spare musket primed? Right; forward the Buffs! Why doesn't that fool pray to Shiva instead of shouting his head off?" he added angrily. "He's only making the lion more excited!"

A row of heads bobbed over the valley lip as he strode forward, and a deep groan of dismay went up as his foot turned on a rounded pebble.

He and Dicky were then only a few feet from the fakir, who had flung himself down on his knees babbling fervent prayers. Fifty yards away the lion was rapidly advancing, leaping the rocks, roaring in anger as it scented its prey.

But as Nicholson's foot slipped, his arms flew wide, his musket clattered to the ground, and he fell heavily on Dicky, who was running forward, the spare gun at the ready, his finger hooked in the trigger-guard. Poor Dick was promptly flattened out, all the breath knocked out of his body, while sharp edges of stone ground into his ribs and knees. His musket went off with a deafening roar, and he sprawled and kicked helplessly, floundering beneath the Deputy Commissioner's enormous weight.

With a last vibrant roar the lion gathered itself together, and leapt with extended claws upon the fakir, who let out a final despairing shriek like an engine's whistle.

John Nicholson was normally agile enough, but his boot had caught in a cranny. As he sat up, tugging with both hands at his ankle, Dicky, feeling he had not a bone unbroken, skittered, crab-fashion, away across the rocks, snatched up Nicholson's musket, and fired it into the tawny body not five feet away. It was a lucky shot: the heavy ball struck and severed the spine a handbreadth behind the head. Without a sound the great cat collapsed on to its side and lay twitching and jerking, while the fakir, with a sound of rending cloth, tore himself free, and fled to the nullah's mouth as though Satan himself were after him.

"Oh, well played, sir!" cried Nicholson, laughing; he was always at his gayest when peril was most imminent. "Good shot, Marvel!"

Freeing his foot with a final jerk, he rose and crossed to Dicky's side.

"Yes, he's done for all right! Lucky for me you kept your wits about you, eh? And for that fakir—hallo, he's disappeared!"

There was a shout of warning from the cliffs, and Nicholson turned sharply and whistled softly.

"There's two of them, Marvel! Look, here comes this brute's mate! Give me that gun!"

"But it's unloaded, sir!" piped Dicky, staring back horror-stricken at where, to their right, a second tawny form had shot raging from the valley bed.

"Never mind! No time for that now! Come on, boy, run, run!"

The Prince was frantically climbing down to meet them, followed by his equerry and the Master of

Horse, but they were fifty yards away, and the
lioness was now roaring at their very heels.

Suddenly Nicholson stopped and faced about,
clubbing his musket over his head, staring defiantly
at his pursuer.

Dicky also stopped, quivering with fright, but
determined not to show it, and Nicholson called
angrily over his shoulder:

"Get away from here at once, Marvel!"

"Please, sir—I'm stopping!" piped Dicky shrilly.

"Do as I order you!"

"I'm sorry, sir, but I can't!" gulped Dicky, staring
helplessly at his useless musket and then at the
lioness, which, suspicious of Nicholson's attitude,
was creeping stealthily towards them.

It seemed to Dicky that an age passed before she
sprang. His teeth chattered, his knees shook, and
the hot sun seemed to bore red-hot pokers into his
brain, and the sour smell of the dead lion and the
hot boulders sickened him. But though he felt
panic-stricken, something kept him rooted to the
spot.

Then the lioness sprang, a living flash of yellow.
Instantly Nicholson struck, and the thud of his blow
startled Dicky into life. He ran up, hitting out feebly
with his own gun, often getting in the Deputy Commissioner's way, whilst the lioness squawled with
fury and pain, and clawed with vicious raking
strokes that once tore the shirt from Nicholson's
mighty shoulders. Roar after angry roar rolled like

thunder across the valley. The watching natives screamed encouragement and delighted admiration. Still the mighty Nikkal Seyn and his slave, the young feringhee, kept the lioness at bay. Her rippling coat was now torn and bloody.

But Dicky was almost finished; panting, the sweat pouring into his eyes and soaking his shirt, though Nicholson still struck, and swayed, and struck again, his musket butt splintered and stained.

Then the Prince ran up, paused, took careful aim, and again the crash of a musket set the vultures hanging in the brazen sky dipping earthwards.

As the lioness rolled over, blood pouring from her mouth and ears, Nicholson threw aside his useless musket, and wiping an arm across his forehead, took Dicky's hand and shook it warmly.

"Did I not tell you he was a warrior, O Prince?" he asked the Rajah.

"Yea, and thou spokest truth," replied the Prince. "He is a shrimp—but a shrimp with a man's stout heart! May Shiva grant such courage to my own eight sons!"

And to Dick's utter amazement the Rajah drew him to him, kissed him, and placed on his finger a small silver ring.

"You see, Marvel," said John Nicholson with a breathless laugh, "there are compensations for taking part in a Roman holiday! Drop to your knee and thank the Prince!"

"What is thy name?" asked the Prince in English,

as Dicky got down awkwardly and pressed his august hand to his sticky forehead.

"Richard Marvel, Your Highness, of Little Paul's Court, London!"

"Marvel of Polly's Court? My servants are yours to command whenever you may wish it! And now let us return to the palace for a bathe and refreshments!"

Hunters set to work to skin the great cats—the lion measured nearly seven feet from nose to tail-tip, and it and its mate each weighed close on three hundred pounds apiece—Dicky and John Nicholson climbed into the empty howdah, and the Rajah led the way back to his palace, up a wide avenue flanked by walnut and deodar trees.

Chapter Eight

THE RAJAH ENTERTAINS

THE PALACE was huge, rambling and cool, its echoing corridors walled with the famous enamelled tiles of the Sindh in gay patterns of turquoise blue, purple, white, and mustard yellow. Bowing slaves led the Deputy Commissioner and Dicky to a suite of large rooms in one wing, whose latticed windows looked out upon gardens bright with flowers and fountains sparkling in the sun. Near at hand was the "bath" of the palace, where, after the Prince had washed himself, guards threw open iron gates, revealing to Dicky's bulging eyes a small swimming-pool set flush with a floor of bright mosaic.

"I'll go first," said Nicholson, taking off his coat. "Will you take my valise into my bedroom next door and lay out my full dress uniform?"

"At once, sir," said Dicky, saluting. "Do you think, sir," he asked wistfully, "I might borrow one of your hairbrushes later?"

Nicholson looked up with a whimsical smile.

"Don't bother about what you will look like, Marvel. Those slaves will take care of you!"

And he indicated three low-caste Hindus standing quietly in a corner, one of whom had a brightly coloured native robe thrown over his arm.

"You don't mean, sir," began Dicky in horror, "I've got to rig myself up in that thing?"

But Nicholson only laughed, and pushed him into

the bedroom, which also had a low door opening on
the "bath."

Dicky unpacked the valise, nervously watching the
three Hindus, who had solemnly filed in after him,
and now stood impassively by the bed. The moment
he had finished laying out the Deputy Commissioner's uniform, sword and cap, they hurled
themselves upon him.

In vain he yelled and struggled. They stripped him
of his clothes, wrapped a loin-cloth deftly round his
waist, and thrust him out into the bathroom, where,
stubbing his toe against the tiles, he did a kind of
exaggerated sword-dance, wildly waving his arms,
beating off despairingly a bevy of large-eyed bath
girls, who drew him gently to the pool.

"Mr. Nicholson, sir! Help!" he bawled shrilly.
"I won't be washed by a lot of girls! A-owg-
grhwohw!"

The tallest girl had slipped behind him and
prodded him neatly in the small of his back, whereupon he plunged headlong into the water, which
was about four feet deep.

As he came up spluttering and gasping, the girls
waded in after him, perfumed soap-balls in their
hands, and, seizing his large ears, used them as
handles whilst they scrubbed and lathered his bony
figure.

"Now, Marvel," said Nicholson, thrusting a
towsled head over the door, "don't make such a
noise! The Rajah will think you're being murdered!"

"They're rubbing scent in my hair!" wailed Dicky dismally. "A-OW-grhwowh!"

But when, an hour later, arrayed in an old but clean pair of the Deputy Commissioner's trousers—very loose round the waist, and very much turned up at the bottom—a trailing blue silk robe and yellow native slippers, scrubbed and anointed till he shone, Dicky sat down to dinner with the Prince and his court, John Nicholson at his side, the banquet that followed more than compensated for all his trials.

The Rajah was dressed in white satin, an osprey plume and a great jewel set in his turban, priceless rings on his fingers, and a rope of lustrous pearls wound four times round his throat. His court was resplendent in blue and scarlet and cloth of gold, with ivory hilted daggers and damascened sword scabbards. Every one squatted on thick brightly coloured mats with little tables inlaid with mother-of-pearl before them; a peacock strutted across the marble floor, whilst against the fluted onyx pillars stood tall troopers of the Prince's Household Guard in uniforms of white and silver, long lances with gaudy swallow-tailed pennants in their hands. But John Nicholson in his quiet, frogged uniform and riding-boots dominated them all. From an ornate iron grille set high in the wall behind, Dicky caught a rustling and chattering as of swallows in the eaves, as the invisible beauties of the Rajah's harem crowded to peep down at the mighty figure of their famous guest.

His mind, however, was wholly set on food. As a trumpet blew, slaves filed in, bearing on gold platters roasted mutton, chickens, and water-fowl, smothered in rich sauces; immense bowls of curry, and salad, and rice mixed with grated fish, goat flesh stewed with barley and walnuts, other dishes which Dicky did not recognise but which gave off a succulent and delicious steam, jars of a dozen kinds of pickles, curdled milk, cream, conserves of fruit, cakes drowned in honey, pastries and tarts, and baskets creaking with luscious grapes, plums, pears, pineapples, gilded oranges, apples, and native fruits; while to drink there was iced sherbet, iced fruit essence in tall frosted glasses, and tawny and dusty and smoky wines in goat-skins and wickered covered flasks and tall bottles of green and yellow and blue glass of native workmanship. Dicky, of course, kept to the iced sherbet, whilst Nicholson never drank anything except water.

As deft slaves placed bowls and plates before him, Dicky fell to with a will, not at all upset by the absence of forks, and blissfully aware that since he knew only a few words of Hindu, he did not need to bother about providing polite conversation. After a few glorious mouthfuls, he paused, reflected, and giggled.

"What amuses the youth?" inquired the Prince of John Nicholson.

"P-please, sir," said Dicky, "I'm ever so sorry. But I just thought that this feed is what Mr. Sykes—

Private Sykes, sir—used to call 'a good blow-out for nowt!'"

John Nicholson gravely explained the joke to the Prince, who did not quite understand it, but taking it as a form of compliment—which indeed it was—laughed, and looked on Dicky with approval.

Towards the end of the meal, Dicky, having stuffed himself, came to the regretful conclusion he really couldn't manage anything more. He therefore topped off with a snack of a lump of sugar cake garnished with honey, clotted cream, and plums, washed it down with a long draught of sherbet—and promptly got a bad attack of hiccups.

"I'm so sorry, sir," he said frantically to John Nicholson. "I really—hic!—am! HIC! I don't know what you'll think of my manners, sir! HIC!"

But among many of the races in India, the highest compliment that can be paid to a host is to be seized with hiccups—it shows that the guest has so enjoyed his food he has eaten to repletion.

The Prince therefore waved away John Nicholson's apologies, and remarked approvingly, "I understand why thou hast chosen the youth as thy slave. He has been well brought up!" And with a smile at Dick, who was blushing crimson with confusion, and almost choking in his efforts to stop the hiccups—clapped his hands loudly. Slaves bore away the dishes returning with silver bowls in which the company washed their fingers, and a native orchestra entered, seating themselves after bowing low to the Rajah.

A troupe of slim girls then performed a native dance, followed by a tall juggler who played with razor-edged daggers till Dick's eyes bulged again out of his head. More music followed, and a bard arose, and sweeping his slender fingers across a guitar, broke into a chant praising the Rajah and his famous guest. Torches flared in sconces against the walls, and when the bard had finished, the Prince beckoned to the Treasurer of the Household, who fee'd the entertainers with showers of silver. As the juggler, bowing low, glanced at John Nicholson, he too drew out some coins, and handed them to the native.

"And now," said the Rajah, "a word in thy ear, O Nikkal Seyn!" He spoke in English, rising to his feet, and at the signal his court salaamed and with bows also to Nicholson, withdrew.

"Let us walk in the garden," said the Rajah, leading the way out into the lofty cloisters.

Dicky's head was nodding, but he rose stiffly to his feet. John Nicholson however bent and whispered, "Get to bed, now, youngster. See my pistols are oiled and loaded before you turn in!"

"Do you wish the boy to attend you, Nikkal Seyn?" asked the Prince, pausing.

Nicholson shook his head.

"It will not be necessary—in thy palace, O Prince of Mangrulkar," he added grimly.

The Rajah bent his head in acknowledgment of the compliment, and walked on, followed by Nicholson.

As their shadows flickered down the cloisters, two
of the tallest guards stepped out after them, side by
side.

Out in a fragrant dusk, where nightingales sang
from rose trees, the Rajah paused by the brink of an
ornamental pool.

"The Ranee, Princess Katishahn, informs me that
that one-eyed fakir whose life ye saved this afternoon
crept into my household at dawn!   He bore a bag of
chupattis, some of which he distributed with these
words: 'Send one to the north, one to the south,
one to the east, and one to the west.   Lo, sub lal
hojaega!' (Everything shall become red!) Know ye
the meaning of this riddle?"

John Nicholson shook his head thoughtfully.

"No, but this is not the first time I have heard
the tale. What has happened to the chupattis?"

"The Ranee, who is my ear and my very dear
guide, does not know, but from what her maid says,
thinks they have been eaten or given away. Those
which the fakir had on him were torn away by the
lion. I saw the bag on the ground, and crushed its
contents with my foot!"

"And the fakir?"

"I have banished him from my estates!"

John Nicholson raised his eyebrows.

"You are a brave man, Prince Premchand of
Mungrelkar. What if your Brahmin hears of this?"

The Rajah smiled faintly in the gloom.

"A tiresome fellow. I think I shall have to send

him on a pilgrimage, so that he can gain merit for us both. Before we met this afternoon he made a fuss over the trout caught for to-night's supper, saying that the largest contained the reincarnated soul of my great-grandmother. However, I pointed out that she gave her life to bring my grandfather into the world, and thus should be proud to gain merit by once again dying to ensure the life of our family. He knows all about the fakir—indeed, I suspect that it was at his invitation that he came here."

"Did he know that I was coming too?" asked Nicholson.

"I imagine so." The Rajah peered up at a huge crimson rose. "No doubt he stopped me going down into that nullah in order that you, being alone, might be killed by the lion. But he cannot complain that I have treated the fakir without due respect!"

"Indeed?" observed Nicholson inquiringly.

"No," said the Rajah. "How delicious is the scent of this bloom! No, I offered the fakir a fair choice between a great reward and banishment. I told him that, if he wished, I would fill his mouth with gold— hot, molten gold, pressed down and running over— but he chose to depart. But since I put no pressure on him to accept either, the Brahmin could not object!"

John Nicholson broke into a low laugh of keen enjoyment.

"O Prince Premchand of Mangrulkar," he said

admiringly, "how wise and subtle thou art! This is a tale that will delight the Governor, who shall certainly hear what a true friend thou art!"

"A pity all you feringhees are not so astute," sighed the Rajah, picking another rose and letting it fall carelessly into the pool. "My master Gulab Singh is sore distressed by the behaviour of these stupid young officers in Srinagar. That is why thou travellest there, is it not?"

"Yes," said Nicholson in astonishment. "But how do you know? It is less than a week since I left Peshawar!"

"Never ask a Hindu a direct question, Nikkal Seyn, or he will confound thee with elaborations and disputations to the hundredth degree. Let it stand that we know, as we know also of the defeats the feringhees have suffered in Russia and Persia—aye, and on these frontiers. Many there be that ask, 'Why should such weak ones rule us any longer?' pointing out that here in India sepoy regiments have won many of such victories as ye can count. Therefore, Nikkal Seyn, deal sternly with those in Srinagar and Kashmir who have shamed your good name and our ancient customs, lest red coats drift down the rivers as those blood-red petals float upon the pool. See how the hungry fish drag down the fair bloom! Keep strict watch, and let thy hand never leave thy sword-hilt, for hungry mouths menace thee. More I may not, cannot say, but as a Ker-lis-ti-an priest (the Rajah meant a Christian missionary) once said to me, 'Watch and pray, for ye know not the hour nor the day!' 'Tis a good motto for such as thou and I, who love this rich ancient land, and would see it prosperous and happy, not torn by cruel wars!"

It was in a thoughtful mood John Nicholson returned to the palace with his host, who, as they approached, began chatting in Hindu for the benefit of spies about land and hut taxes, and similar domestic affairs.

Dicky was awakened in the morning by John Nicholson cheerily singing "John Peel" as he splashed in the bath. Hurriedly rising, he was polishing the Deputy Commissioner's sword-belt when he returned.

"'Fraid I'm late this morning, sir," Dicky began, but Nicholson smiled.

"Most lads of your age would be, after fighting that lion yesterday. Many thanks for helping me!"

After breakfast they took a ceremonial farewell of their host, who waived the usual custom of his class, which is to spend the morning with their astrologers. The Prince had provided a glittering escort of fifteen picked troopers of his Guard, all of them well over six feet in height, and they clattered out of the palace amid great excitement, the court ministers and servants running to the gates with bows and deep salaams.

"We shan't be riding along any of Lord Dalhousie's excellent new roads for some time, Marvel," John Nicholson observed after a while.

"Oh, are we going into the forest, sir?" asked Dicky.

The Deputy Commissioner shook his head.

"The monsoon is just beginning, and the trees will be full of leeches, horrid fat things that fasten on your neck. No, we are going by boat!"

And so it proved. Riding through a heavy shower of rain along the fringe of the forest, they came at dusk to the mighty river Jhelum, swirling along as it neared the narrows at Baramulla. The escort had ridden away at noon, and they stopped for the night at a little khan, or inn. In the morning they and their horses stepped aboard a flat-bottomed barge manned by eight brown-skinned Bhils. A mast was stepped as they pushed off into the yellow tide, but the mountains on either side cut off all but fitful puffs of wind.

Nevertheless, the eight oarsmen, keeping to the sides, where the current was not so strong, made good progress up stream, rhythmically digging in their paddles to an endless monotonous chant.

John Nicholson sat in the bows, wrapped in thought, occasionally raising his hand in acknowledgment of the salutes from those on the banks or on passing craft who recognised him.

Dicky sat in the stern, gazing open-mouthed around him as the smoking mists of the morning vanished from the river's face, revealing a teeming pageant of crowded colourful life.

Fishermen prowled in native canoes, and there

were barges laden deep with salt and hides and silk,
surging down on the current to the various wharves
along the banks. Long, narrow boats with curved
prows and stems, painted red and blue and yellow,
bore travellers like themselves, and once or twice the
galley of a lesser Rajah, its awnings gay with
bright-coloured silks, banners and pennants streaming, musicians playing on its decks, glided by.
Herons stood motionless in the shallows, and gaily
coloured duck, and other water fowl, rose from the
river with shrill cries. Through the trees of the pine
forests stepped stately ibex, ooriel, and Kashmir
stags, to drink at the brink, thundering away with
a flash of startled hooves as fat brown and black
bears rolled down from the hill slopes which
stretched up and up, heaving the forests like a shaggy
mantle on their shoulders, till far above the icy
peaks glittered in the morning sun.

Here and there were green clearings in the forests,
filled by busy villages, by crude houses on wooden
piles, the homes of primitive tribes such as the Bhils,
the Juangs, and the Todas, or by quaint rose-pink
and saffron-yellow temples, pagodas, and statues of
Buddha or Hindu gods.

The roads that occasionally dipped along the
river's brink were crowded with bullock carts, long
trains of heavily laden camels—caravans passing
from Ladak and Kashmir to Turkestan—foot
travellers, and strings of ponies led by Afghan horse
dealers. Once or twice a score of "walers"—raw

Australian horses for the cavalry of the Rajah's armies—appeared, led by troopers in uniforms of white and silver. Dicky, who had never seen them before, was especially attracted by the Tibetan lamas who trudged along indifferent to the dust and sudden fierce showers, telling their beads and chanting hour-long prayers.

As the mighty ranges thrown off from the peak of Nanga Parbat drew back, they passed into a broad valley where the river widened to the lake of Wular. The dense forests of birch and maple, pine and fir, receded behind broad fields of vivid green where bare-legged natives sowed their summer crops of rice, and Indian corn.

"Enjoying yourself, Marvel?" asked a lazy voice.

Dicky looked round with a start, to see John Nicholson had turned and was quietly watching him with a quizzical air. His right elbow rested on a thwart, and in his hand he held a paper-covered book.

"By jingo, yes, sir," said Dicky shrilly. "Reminds me of the Lowther Arcade[1] on Saturday afternoon!"

Nicholson laughed with keen appreciation.

"Not such a bad description at that," he remarked. "Many of the shawls and carpets, jewels, turquoises, and copper vessels they sell there come from these parts! You will see the shops in Srinagar and Kashmir. But the natives were making them long before the Lowther Arcade was built. Caravans, like that one over there, were carrying them down over

[1] A famous Victorian London bazaar—*Author*.

the plains and up through those mountains into Tibet and China centuries before London existed! Alexander, the great Greek general, came as far as this, and the river was called Mydaspes by Greek historians and geographers. There are natives living here called Khans who trace their descent to those long-dead Greeks. Oh, it's a strange country, Kashmir, and unbelievably ancient!"

"Is that a history book you have been reading, sir?"

"This?" John Nicholson held up the paper-back volume with a smile. "Oh, no. It's a novel, *Dombey and Son*, by a very great writer, Charles Dickens. He's a wonderful man, and I expect will still be read when we are forgotten!"

Laying the book down, he called to the native headman.

"It's afternoon already, and that looks like a nasty squall coming up," pointing out a black cloud to Dicky. "We're still over twenty miles from Srinagar, so I think we'll pull in, and try and find accommodation at the local zemindar's[1] house!"

[1] Country squire—*Author*.

Chapter Nine

THE BROKEN TWIG

THE STORM burst with the swift fury of a monsoon before they reached the bank. The craft on the lake were blotted out by grey sheets of rain that hissed and beat upon them like hail, while the sky turned black and purple, and jagged by white vicious streaks of blinding lightning. The thunder was incessant, rolling among the mountain peaks, and the two horses in the waist of the boat became restless, whinnying and stamping on the boards. As two of the native oarsmen leapt overside to tug the barge into the shallows, Dicky, attempting to soothe Nicholson's charger, was almost kicked after them. The brute plunged and reared, and as in answer to a shout from Nicholson, he loosed its halter, it charged for the bank, dragging his own pony after it, and soaking him to the skin in showers of muddy river water. Peal after peal of deafening thunder reverberated across the fields, but Dicky, grimly struggling to control the great black horse and the pony, managed to get them under the rough shelter of a bamboo shed, already crowded with peasants scurrying in out of the storm. As he called to the Bhils to help, a familiar figure appeared at his elbow.

"Give them to me, feringhee!" said Dev Sahai with a grin. "So-ho, my pretty creatures! Hush then, do not be frightened!"

"Why, hallo, Dev," piped Dicky. "I say, be a sport, and hang on a moment, will you? I must go and help Mr. Nicholson!"

Dev nodded, stroking the charger's nose, and in the expressive phrase of horsemen, "making much of it," the pony trustfully nuzzling at his shoulder, while Dick ran back to the boat, meeting John Nicholson striding up the path, valises and portfolios tucked under his arms, musket and sword slung over his shoulder.

"Help the Bhil headman to get the awning up, will you, Marvel?" he asked.

Drenched and dripping, they gathered again in the shed, where Dev had secured the horses to a post. His intended salaam was broken off as the Deputy Commissioner shook his hand warmly.

"'Tis perhaps as well," Dev remarked in a low voice. "There are thugs not far away who would laugh with glee to know that thou art here alone!"

"Oh, dear," said Nicholson. "Not more people thirsting for my blood? It's really becoming most tiresome!"

"Thou art pleased to jest," replied Dev with an answering flash of white teeth, "but there be many in these borders upon whose sons or husbands thy hand has fallen heavily! Others, too, who do not forget that the charge of thy soldiers, led by thee, shattered the ranks of the Sikh army, broke up their empire, and made of Kashmir a separate state! And others yet again who remember that thou and Mr. Edwardes have placed a Hindu to rule a land of Moslems!"

"Terribly difficult to please everyone," murmured Nicholson, shaking the water from his cap, "but though Gulab Singh the Rajput reigns over a population ninety per cent of whom are Moslems, what of Hyderabad, O learned one, where a Moslem rules over a population ninety per cent of whom are Hindus? Eh, young feller?"

"You are laughing at me," said Dev sourly. "Come to the caravan, mighty one, and my uncle shall confound thee!"

"I wondered if he were about. You came down to catch those fish, hm?"

Dev nodded, and held up a string of fine fat trout.

"Take supper with us, and ye shall taste them."

"Catch 'em with a worm?" inquired Dicky enviously.

"No, these bits of red cloth," and Dev held out some scraps of linen. "We are journeying down to Turkestan, and have many bales of fine cotton and wool!"

"I would like to sup with you and your uncle," said Nicholson. "Please give him my salaams. But we are on business of the Company, and must push on! When you return, if your traffic takes you across the plains of the Punjab, do not fail to come and see me—and Marvel, too!"

As Dev made for the door, waving farewells, Nicholson said to Dicky, "Try and keep up your friendship with Dev, Marvel. He's a fine strapping chap, with plenty of sense in his head. Listen to all he has to say too—he's no fool, and a lot of gossip comes to his ears as he travels about the country-side!"

"He gave that priest an awful savage look, sir," replied Dicky, indicating an old Tibetan lama who sat in the corner, drawing designs in the mud amid a breathless circle of coolies.

"Yes, as a good Mussulman he regards all other religions with scorn," replied Nicholson, turning to gaze at the lama. "Do you see what the old man is sketching with that twig he holds?"

Putting his hand on Dicky's shoulder, he stepped across with him to the intent circle.

"Looks like a wheel, sir," said Dicky.

"Most probably it is," returned Nicholson. "The Tibetans believe that life is an endless wheel, in which men and women pass through many strange changes. Probably he is explaining it to the natives!"

The weary old eyes of the lama were upon them as they approached, dark pools that held all knowledge and for whom life held no more mysteries. Slowly they turned from Dicky to the graceful strength of the Deputy Commissioner, then his face broke into a thousand wrinkles as he smiled gently at Dicky, beckoning him to approach.

At the same time he made signs to the circle of coolies that they were to withdraw, and they crept back against the flimsy bamboo walls whilst the rain hissed down outside.

"He thinks you are my 'chela'—disciple," whispered Nicholson to Dicky. "Like that young man there"—nodding to a novitiate with a shaven head, who sat wrapped in a yellow robe, his eyes closed, a wooden begging bowl in his lap, against the wall behind the lama. "He would like to draw your horoscope—tell your fortune," he went on, listening intently to the lama's sibilant dialect. "When were you born?"

The old man slowly drew a wheel in the dust of the floor, and John Nicholson interpreted for Dicky, explaining how the stars influenced his present life, and how he would pass onward round the wheel to adventures and experiences yet undreamt of.

"You will see great battles," the lama gazed up at Dicky with a strange far-away look. "You will approach near to death, know triumph and disaster, and great sorrow. But out of sorrow shall come happiness and a message, and ye shall hearken to the message, and live to find the supreme happiness of service for others!"

The lama bent, and swept away the picture with a gnarled finger.

"And now he is going to cast my horoscope," whispered Nicholson.

Slowly the twig began to trace a circle, but ere it was complete, there came a terrible crash of thunder right over the roof of the shed. The lama's disciple did not even open his eyes, but the coolies crouched down with cries of terror. The lama paused abruptly, and Dicky, staring down with a chill stab of horror, saw that the twig was broken, and the circle trailed off meaninglessly into the dust.

Again the lama slowly raised his head, and his eyes met the Deputy Commissioner's, who stood rigid, gazing at him. Some unspoken message seem to pass between them. One or two of the coolies crawled forward, chattering excitedly as they saw the broken twig and the unfinished circle.

Then the lama's head sank once more upon his breast, and he began to run his beads through his fingers, sonorously chanting, " *Ho mane padme hum,*" a solemn prayer in which his chela, still without opening his eyes, joined in, in a low voice.

"Poof, it's hot in here," said Nicholson. "The rain is ceasing, Marvel. Let's get out into the open, shall we?"

"Sir," said Dicky, "that broken circle——"

"Oh, an old wives' tale," laughed the Deputy Commissioner, but his laugh did not ring true. "If you think it means anything, better keep your weather eye lifting for those thugs Dev mentioned!"

Just a silly accident, an old wives' tale, as the Deputy Commissioner rightly described it; so Dicky tried to convince himself. How ridiculous to imagine that anything could happen to John Nicholson, a man not yet forty, in the prime of life. But nevertheless he felt uneasy all day, and at night his sleep was disturbed by dreams forgotten when he awoke.

They took boat again after breakfast, and by noon

were approaching the ancient town of Srinagar with its seven wooden bridges across the river. On both banks poor native huts huddled against stone and brick warehouses, interspaced with lovely gardens and the villas of rich merchants. Hindu temples jostled statues of Buddha, where yellow robed priests laid flowers on the idol's feet, and from minarets came the cry of the muezzins summoning the faithful to prayer.

"*La ilahah ill Allah, Mohammed Rasoul Allah.*" (There is no God but Allah, and Mohammed is his prophet.)

From behind bead curtains and worm-eaten wooden lattices came the clack of the silk-weavers' looms, and the clink-clink of the hammers of bronze and copper and silver smiths. Here and there the embankments were almost level with the river, and stagnant pools lay in the poorer streets, together with piles of stinking garbage; whilst at one point Hindu burning ghats, where the dead were cremated, smoked and fumed sullenly.

"Cremation is a most sensible custom in these hot climates," John Nicholson observed as they rowed past. "But we've done one good thing in India, we've stopped widows burning themselves alive with their husbands!"

"Is that what they called Suttee, sir?" Dicky asked.

"Satis is the actual word," said Nicholson. "A horrible, cruel, custom it was, too. No matter how young she was, a young Hindu wife had to build a

funeral pyre for her dead husband, and, when it was
alight, cast herself on top. But since 1842 the East
India Company has stamped it out. The Ghurkas in
the adjoining state of Nepal are much more sensible.
They are Hindus, but much kinder to their women
folk. They marry little girls to the bel fruit, which
is then cast into a stream and allowed to float away.
When the girls grow up, and marry in earnest,
should their husbands die, they can't burn themselves
with him, because the bel fruit has been lost.
Ingenious idea, isn't it?"

"The Ghurkas are friendly to us, are they, sir?"

John Nicholson nodded and smiled.

"Yes, fortunately, for they are terrible fighters.
A war with Tibet only ended two years back, in their
victory, and they've been scrapping with China for
centuries. Their native weapon is a heavy, curved,
short sword, called a kukri. They shave with it, peel
potatoes with it, lop off an enemy's head with it at
one blow, eat with it, sleep with it! You may see
some of them in Kashmir—Srinagar is too full of
fever for us to stop here—for we are building up a
big native force of Ghurkas and Rajputs, the fighting
Hindus of Kashmir state. That's why we've come to
these parts. Some of the younger white officers sent
to drill the natives have been getting up to mischief
—painting the sacred cows in the streets with blue
and red paint, and similar nonsense. It sounds rather
funny to us, but the Hindus are furious. Gulab
Singh, the Amir, sent to Mr. Edwardes personally,

asking for me to come along and stop the idiots, so—
here we are!"

Gulab Singh, the Rajput or warrior Hindu who
had been made Amir of Kashmir by the East India
Company after the last Sikh war, had retired to a
palace in the hills, leaving the valleys which, during
the monsoon months of June to September, are full
of fever and cholera.

So Dicky was left in the barracks of the native
army at Kashmir, while John Nicholson rode up
into the mountains to visit him. There were no
white soldiers of his own age or rank to speak to,
but the Deputy Commissioner installed him in a
house under care of a Moslem scribe, with whom he
studied native dialects. At night he wandered out
through the bazaars, watching the teeming life that
poured through the narrow streets. He saw the
Ghurkas Nicholson had mentioned, short thick-set
jolly men; many with their eyebrows partly shaved
as a mark of respect for relatives who had died in the
recent campaign against Tibet; Moslem merchants,
Afghan horsedealers, and the native Kashmiri, poor
down-trodden folk, their national spirit crushed by
the successive invasions that had poured over their
edge of the world. He also saw one or two senior
white officers; the subalterns were confined to their
quarters at night until Nicholson had dealt with
them.

Chapter Ten

THE SWORD AND THE BIBLE

THERE was so much to see, so much to do and learn, that when John Nicholson returned, Dicky was quite surprised to learn that over a week had gone by.

The Deputy Commissioner was accompanied by a tall thin gentleman, clean shaven except for a fringe of ginger whiskers framing his sharp features, whom Dicky learnt was Mr. William Price, a regimental surgeon attached to the native troops, and who had been attending the Amir who, a month previous, had been taken slightly ill.

"Preposterous affair," remarked Mr. Price. "Stomach-ache resulting from too much curdled milk and pickles. I thought he wanted me for something spectacular—a bold bit of surgery that would impress his native pill-rollers!"

"In this heat?" inquired John Nicholson dryly.

"Oh, he'd certainly have got gangrene," replied Mr. Price airily. "Still, it would have been a good bit of practice. Fancy being able to advertise when I get home that I attended the Prince of Kashmir! Why, my surgery would have been crowded— crowded, sir!"

He paused and regarded Dicky with a speculative frown.

"So this is the young prodigy! Hm, he'd be invaluable to an anatomy class—every bone distinct! He advanced and held out his hand. "How do you do, Mr. Marvel? And how are all the poor Peruvians?"

"The poor Peruvians, sir?" piped Dicky, greatly puzzled.

"Yes, the poor fellows have been without pocket handkerchiefs for twenty-five years—twenty-five years, just imagine it!" said Mr. Price, who was something of a wag. "Mr. Nicholson, since you will be interviewing those young fools for the next hour or two, I'll take care of Mr. Marvel. He can help make up the medicine for that village where they've got the cholera! Convenient?"

"Quite," said Nicholson. "It's a good opportunity for him to pick up a bit of useful knowledge!"

"I have never been able to decide whether the medical profession is composed of fools or saints," remarked Mr. Price, leading the way into a large dispensary, redolent of rhubarb and senna, where native orderlies were mixing drugs on slate topped tables. "Either they are heroes, devoting themselves to the service of humanity, or idiots trying to do themselves out of work by curing all the sick people. Very bad business to cure your patients, you know! They don't think you've done anything unless they've nearly died! And if you let them get very sick, they usually do die, and that's bad for business too. Most distressing!" He took a pinch of snuff.

"Fetch those stone jars over here, and pour that mixture into 'em. Chalk and opium—that's the stuff to scotch the cholera! Usually kills the patient too, but man can but do his best. *'Tis not in man's nature to demand success, but we'll do more, we will deserve it!* Know who wrote that?"

"Shakespeare, sir," piped Dicky, who had once heard the lines at a play.

"Well, well," said Mr. Price, taking another pinch of snuff. "A drummer boy who knows Shakespeare. A veritable Solomon in embryo. Don't upset that stuff in the black jar! It's blister ointment—take the skin off your elbow like one o'clock!" He banged down a large pestle and mortar on the table. "When you've finished bottling that stuff, pound up this mixture—and don't go tasting it—it contains ginger, ipecacuanha, cinchona bark, and epsom salts—the results would surprise you. It's a special secret mixture of my own. I made my reputation on it—guaranteed to cure anything, from pimples to the itch!"

Dicky glanced at the shelf above his head, where a clumsy brass microscope pitted with damp stood under a large glass jar with a big knob on the top.

"Don't tell me you know what that is!" exclaimed Mr. Price. "Why, my own profession loathe the sight of the beastly thing! It's lenses have revealed that one cherished medical fad after another is utterly without foundation. And there was a man at my old hospital, St. Bartholomew's, who wrote a book on Infusoria-microscopic water life, in which he suggested that fevers and inflammations may be caused by invisible animalcular life. His name was

Gideon Mantell—he was a famous scientist as well as a rattling good surgeon—died about four years ago, I've a got copy of his book, though many surgeons say it ought to be burnt publicly at Smith-field.   Fancy suggesting that illness is caused by germs of invisible life!   Did you ever hear such nonsense? But of course," he took another pinch of snuff, staring meaningly at Dicky, "there *might* be something in it, don't you think?"

He stalked away to attend to two natives who had just nervously crept in, and Dicky began decanting the sticky black liquid into the flasks. Suddenly a piercing yell rent the air. Dicky nearly dropped the jar and turned round to see Mr. Price triumphantly flourishing a large tooth held in a kind of screw-wrench over his head.

"What a beauty!" he shouted. "Got it first shot!"

There was another yell from the second native, who with one horrified glare at the surgeon, rushed for the open door. But Mr. Price jerked out his leg, and as his patient sprawled headlong, dropped on to his back, calling to the native orderlies to help. More deafening shrieks followed, then Mr. Price rose beaming to his feet, dusting his hands, while the luckless natives groaned and stared at each other in dismay.

"A nasty little subluxation of the carpo-metacarpal phalangeal joint," said the surgeon breathlessly, "but I fixed it!"

He whipped a bandage round the injured wrist,

stiffened it with an application of gum from a large gallipot, and then stood back. The wretched patients, realising they were free, stampeded for the door, collided heavily, and disappeared outside as if a mad dog were at their heels.

"Hm, they never even thanked me," remarked Mr. Price bitterly, and disappeared with an injured air into his office.

Dicky finished decanting the cholera mixture, smelt his fingers dubiously, and began grinding the powders in the mortar. After an hour Mr. Price appeared, bearing a large wooden box lined with red velvet and containing a fearful set of bone-handled instruments, which he gave one of the orderlies to clean. Then he strolled over to Dicky, took another pinch of snuff, and leant conversationally against the bench.

"I'm one of the blessings of civilisation," he announced. "Lord Dalhousie, who leaves us this year, was an excellent Governor. He not only built excellent roads, projected the Ganges canal and three trunk railways, instituted a legislative council for all India at Calcutta—the nearest approach to Bedlam I've ever struck—but also founded schools, and dispensaries like this one. As you saw just now, however, we are never appreciated. Great is the harvest, but the labourers never get any thanks. Not that I, personally, expect gratitude—philanthropy is always misunderstood! Hallo, there are those young cubs coming out of John Nicholson's office! Look just as though a mine had burst under 'em!"

Dicky looked through the tall arched windows to see five white-faced subalterns creeping down the veranda steps, feebly mopping their brows. Without a word to each other, they separated, and moved away across the dusty parade ground, their backs eloquent of utter woe.

A moment later John Nicholson strode briskly into the pharmacy.

"You talked to 'em like a father, eh?" remarked Mr. Price dryly.

"I've no patience with fools," Nicholson frowned. "High spirits are natural enough, but to insult native customs might start a war. As I said to them, how would they like it if Indians conquered Britain, and came to jeer at our church services, and painted the crucifixes red and blue? Ensign Dent I shall send home. His life is in danger since he tried to snatch off a high-born Hindu lady's veil, and in any case I have no use for men of his type—lazy, insolent, and intemperate!"

"You think there might be a revolt?"

John Nicholson shrugged his mighty shoulders.

"I hope not. I think the border is quiet enough, on the whole, but there are some odd rumours flying round!"

Mr. Price took a large pinch of snuff. "Watch the Oudh, that's my advice. The tukaldars[1] are furious

[1] Feudal barons—*Editor*.

that the Company has stopped their Saturday afternoon amusements of looting and torturing, and
Lucknow is a sink, full of lazy parasites and treacherous officials out of work. That, in my opinion,
is the focal spot, ahem, of a possible future fever!"

"Which can only be cured by the good old custom
of blood-letting, eh?" said Nicholson grimly. "Well,
we shall see!"

Mr. Price came with them when two days later
John Nicholson led the way out of the town, and
headed south, across the river Chenab and through
the Swalik hills into the Punjab.

There he left them to travel on to Lucknow, whilst
Dicky and the Deputy Commissioner spent the hot
summer in paying a round of visits to the great Sikh
Maharajahs, and the lesser Rajahs and zemindars,[1]
from Patiala across the barren central plains to
Amritsar and Lahore. At noon the sun was so fierce
they had to rest for two or three hours, and so they
would rise at dawn, jogging off in the mists through
gloomy mountain passes, fording swift torrents,
stumbling up rocky paths, or cantering off by
plantations of bamboo and shisham across flat sandy
deserts dotted by scrub, where peasants struggled to
grow patches of corn, oats, and maize. In the cool
of the evening, when rocks and sand reflected heat
like a furnace door, they would approach some fort
perched on a crag, or a rambling palace built of pink
or yellow stone. In the hues of sunset, the forts

[1] Country squires—*Editor.*

appeared like toy castles built of cardboard, turrets and walls standing up against a sky of pearl and orange and gold, whilst in the gardens of the palaces native flowers and roses gave out a delicious perfume. They met with some adventures, for there were human bandits—dacoits, and thugs—lurking on the roads, leopards stealing through the forests of deodar and pines, and near the rivers in which they sometimes bathed, crocodiles sunned themselves on the sandy banks.

There was a great deal of work for both of them, for John Nicholson was not merely paying a round of social calls—he was also engaged in inspecting the native troops of the Rajahs—foot soldiers as well as cavalry—in advising the village headmen on the cultivation of their crops—studying the complicated systems of currency—many of the greater princes issued coins of their own within their territory— discussing problems of health with dispensary physicians—and spending many hours talking over political problems with the princes and squires. This last was perhaps his most important duty, for the wounds of the last Sikh war were only just closed, and some of the rajahs tucked away in remote corners and up in the hills still brooded over their defeat, and required tact and firmness from the high official of the East India Company who came to visit them. It says much for the Deputy Commissioner's skill and generous personality that he left none but friends behind him.

Almost every night, except Sundays, Dicky, bone-weary and stifling huge yawns, sat in mud huts or cool palace chambers, writing up, at John Nicholson's dictation, official records and private notes for the personal eye of Mr. Herbert Edwardes and the Governor-General. On Sunday evenings, however, John Nicholson would read aloud the service for the day from the prayer-book he always carried, and sometimes a chapter or two from the New Testament. His was the creed of the old frontier pioners, the Sword and the Bible. Sometimes he would ask Dicky to read, but though Nicholson himself had a simple faith that if he did his duty all would be well, he never preached, nor attempted to convert their hosts, who now and again asked permission to be present. Sitting cross-legged on silk cushions or on mud floors, high-born noble or peasant would listen in absorbed silence as Nicholson translated into their own tongue what had been read.

Afterwards they would ask questions, or discuss points that were not clear, always, even in the village headman's hut or under the counsel tree, with perfect courtesy and good breeding. Not the Brahmin priests, or the Sadhus with the caste mark on their forehead, ever raised their voice, though they did not always agree with the text, and Dicky, watching them, was disagreeably reminded of the greasy, red-nosed "Hot Gospeller" who used to rant in his stepfather's parlour on Sunday afternoons. But once John Nicholson observed to him:

"The religions of India, Marvel, are unhappy ones. They never take a man out of himself. The most any native can hope for is to lose himself in a kind of frozen bewilderment where this world doesn't worry him. That's where Christianity is so different. If you are really trying to help others, you've got no time to bother about yourself and your short-comings! I agree wholeheartedly with Mr. Edwardes belief that until India is leavened with Christianity she will be unfit for freedom, and that when she is, she will be unfit for anything *less*. England may then, he believes, leave the stately daughter she has reared, to walk the future with a free imperial step. It's a wonderful idea, you know. I don't want the natives taught just the ceremonies of religion, hymn singing, and prayers morning and evening. India is split up by dozens of creeds and systems of caste and worship, but if all of them, Sikhs, Rajputs, Hindus, Moslems, Buddhists, could just learn the simple ideal of service for all, service for others, not self, so that they all worked together for the common good, what a mighty country this might become! That's what we're all trying to do now, and that must be your ideal when you succeed us—yes, and of those who come after you, too!"

Living among the land between the Five Rivers, the land of the Sikhs, it was not surprising that Dicky learnt much about them. The Sikh by birth and training is a warrior, and taught from birth to be honest and courageous, truthful and pure, to worship their One God, and to keep faith even to death. He would see, returning from a trip, tall troopers washing waist-long hair, for the Sikh must not cut hair or beard, and his beard is supported by a thin black cord tied round the head. He must bathe frequently, if possible at Amritsar, their Holy City, and always carry weapons, or iron to remind him of them. The initiated Sikh wears five symbols by which he may be distinguished from other Indians, all of which begin with the letter K—Kirpan, the knife, for readiness to fight; Kesh, the uncut hair on which Kanga the comb is used; Kaura, the iron bangle for fidelity; and Kuch, the shorts, for swiftness of foot. An Inner Guard of the Faith, the Akhalis, pile their hair into a pyramid held in position by steel quoits with sharp edges—ugly weapons at close quarters. Such were the men, the horsemen in blue, the infantry in red or buff, all uniforms having red facings, whose regiments John Nicholson inspected, who formed the powerful Punjab Frontier Force, which, seasoned by one or two regiments of white soldiers, kept the peace of the great White Queen Victoria along the roaring frontiers. Warriors all, bred in the tradition of war, who believed the mighty Deputy Commissioner, who had led them in more than one desperate fight, to be the very incarnation of the God of War.

"We would follow him into hell," one ressaldar[1] said simply to Dicky, "for he never cries *Chelo bhai*

[1] A native captain of Indian cavalry—*Author.*

chelo! (Go on, brothers!) but always *Chelo ao, chelo ao*! (Come on, follow me!)"

Upright, honourable, the Sikhs were a contrast to the other great fighting race of India, the Mahrattas, whose rulers had become treacherous and indolent and a startling contrast to the peaceful Jains, who hold that all life is sacred, who will not therefore kill even an insect, and who, it is said, actually had homes of rest for fleas and bugs where from time to time devout pilgrims allowed such pests to have a meal off them.

As the monsoon months drew to a close, Nicholson set his face for Peshawar.

"We can't leave Mr. Edwardes alone at this time of year!" he remarked to Dicky as they rode out from a village early one morning.

"Why, sir?" asked Dicky. "Are you expecting trouble?"

"There is always trouble brewing in the hills in the autumn," said Nicholson with a laugh. "When the harvest is in, the Pathan has nothing to do, so he gets down his musket, and goes out to liven things up. If he hasn't got a feud to polish off, he can always start a new one. And then too, the Proindahs, the Afghan travelling merchants, begin to arrive in Peshawar in the autumn, bringing wool, dyes, poshtins,[1] silks, carpets, gold thread, fruits, precious stones—all manner of attractive things—from Kabul and Bokhara and Samarkand. Naturally enough,

[1] Sheepskin clothes—*Author*.

they're all armed to the teeth—some of them have old scores to wipe off with the native hillmen that cause bloodshed year after year—and they have to have their teeth drawn—leave their weapons with us before they are allowed to take their goods on to Delhi and Agra and Calcutta! And *that* more often than not leads to some very heated arguments!"

Back at Peshawar Dicky was settled on a stool in the office of the "tikki-wallah"—the telegraph clerk. He found the Eighty-Seventh Regiment of Foot in their familiar red coats with blue facings had marched away to the Camp of Exercise in the Euzulfai country, and that the other white regiment of the border force—the Twenty-Fourth Regiment of Foot,[1] whose scarlet tunics had facings of willow green, and whose small shakoes bore a star-shaped plate surmounted by a crown with the regimental number in the centre—had returned from their patrol of the mountains, and settled into the barracks. Every morning he would hear their measured tramp as detachments marched in from the cantonments two miles to the west of the city, and watch them as they filed into the narrow streets —tall, black-browed giants like Corporal Beynon, large clumsy men from Somerset and the Severn valley, dapper little beady-eyed Welshmen, and craggy, stunted men whose fathers were miners in the Mendip hills. Led perhaps by Captain Trevor, or bearded Lieutenant Powys, they would form

[1] Now the South Wales Borderers—*Author*.

guard at the gates, and begin examining the travellers who poured into the city with strings of laden pack-ponies or a dozen haughty camels. It was an unenviable and noisy job; every native considered the examination a bitter insult directed deliberately against himself, and complained loudly and at considerable length. To be disarmed was the last straw, and led more than once to some savage scuffles; Private Davies was knifed in the arm, and a native shot, in one riot. All round the shouting, gesticulating traders, prowled bazaar thieves, watching for opportunities to slit open a bale of goods or snatch a purse; the camels snarled and bit all and sundry, and to make confusion worse, hillmen making a trip to the town would sometimes recognise an old enemy, or be detected themselves by some merchant they had robbed, and more fights would break out. And all this seething, bawling, hot torrent of vivid life was hemmed-in, in narrow twisted streets and alleys where the crowd at times was jammed firmly between the walls. Even when those infantrymen not on duty went to bathe in the evening cool in the river Bara, near whose left bank the town is situated, they had to post a guard to see that their clothes and accoutrements did not disappear. The hill thief is the most impudent and clever in the world.

Chapter Eleven

HYMN TO NIKKAL SEYN

ONE MORNING John Nicholson called Dicky in to dictate some reports to him. They had been working on them for about an hour, when there was the sound of voices outside. The voices grew more insistent, then came the sound of a scuffle, and the door abruptly burst open. The Sikh sentry hurtled headlong into the room, locked in a close grip with a black-robed fakir whose eyes blazed with excitement. As they rolled across the floor, a dozen other fakirs solemnly filed in, stepping across their struggling comrade's body, and seated themselves on the floor with their backs to the wall facing the Deputy Commissioner. One, whose black robes were ornamented with a white and yellow scarf, then gave a signal, and suddenly salaamed until his head rattled against the dusty wooden boards. At once those with him followed suit, throwing themselves flat on their faces, whilst the leader began intoning a deep-throated chant.

Dicky, who had jumped up in alarm, caught some of the words. It appeared to be a hymn of praise to Nicholson, but before it was ended, Nicholson, his face contorted with rage, put a whistle to his lips and blew it loud and long.

The Sikh sentry staggered erect, grimly holding his prize, and dragging him to the door, kicked him outside, calling shrilly for help. But the office had awakened to life at the scream of Nicholson's whistle, and suddenly Mr. Edwardes appeared in the door from the inner office, a pistol cocked ready in his hand. But as his eyes fell on the strange visitors, his anxious look was replaced by one of acute delight, and he burst into roars of laughter, leaning helplessly against the doorpost, and wiping away the tears streaming down his cheeks.

Meantime the hymn appeared to be nearing its end.

"Great and mighty is our Lord and Master Nikkal Seyn!" cried the leader, knocking his head frenziedly against the floor.

"Wallah ahai!" cried the others, waving their arms above their heads. "Powerful as the elephant, fierce as the buffalo, cunning as the mongoose!"

"The tramp of his war horse echoes from Attock to the Khyber, the stamp of his feet rocks the mountains, his eye cleaves the heart like the lightning flash!" went on the leader, and suddenly jumping to his legs, made a dive under the table at Nicholson's feet.

The others followed his example; the table shot into the air, and then went over backwards, whilst Dicky was swept aside by the flailing arms of the Deputy Commissioner, who, caught by surprise, was tipped backwards out of his chair, striking the wall behind with a crash that brought clouds of dust from the ceiling. As a dense mob of heaving bodies, arms, and legs, rolled backwards and forwards across the

room, splintering the furniture, cracking the paint
from the walls, Dicky hastily crawled for safety into
the inner office, whilst Mr. Edwardes roared and
stamped, waggling his head from side to side with
helpless laughter. The building shook; an earth-
quake seemed to convulse the outer office, and John
Nicholson suddenly appeared, like a swimmer coming up for air, whilst from beneath the scrum a
fakir, his robes in tatters, bolted for the door,
flourishing one of the Deputy Commissioner's
boots over his head.

"I have our Lord's boot!" he screamed. "Come,
my brothers, let us depart and build an altar around
it, where all the world can come to wonder and to
pray!"

Several of his companions rushed after him, but
sepoys were now running up outside, and all were
caught. John Nicholson himself, his coat torn, his
hair over his eyes, held the leader under one massive
arm, and shouted, frantic with rage, "Get my boot!
Bring it here at once! Marvel, Chatuwa, Fazir, don't
stand gaping around! Get my boot!"

At length some order was restored, and what
remained of the furniture set on its legs. John
Nicholson, his face white with fury, pulled on his
boot, and wiped off the ink spilt on his chair.

Then he glared up at the leader of the fakirs, who
smiled and smirked back, and would have salaamed
again, only his arms were held tightly by two
stalwart sepoys.

"I have told you before," thundered Nicholson, "I will have no more of this nonsense! There is but one God, he whom I worship, Jesus Christ the Nazarene. Pay your devotions to Him, not to me, who am but His poor servant. I warned you if you persisted in this blasphemous foolery my hand would be heavy! Take them out, all of them, and flog them!"

As the sepoys dragged them away, every member of the deputation struggling to turn and smile back adoringly at Nicholson, he sat back, and smoothed down his glossy hair.

"Idiots!" he muttered, then caught sight of Mr. Edwardes, grinning as he departed, and smiled sheepishly at Dicky. "Fakirs of Hazara," he explained, settling his collar. "Renounced their own Asiatic god to make one of me![1] Did you ever hear of such cheek?"

[1] A sect was actually founded as described. The last member dug his own grave and was found dead in it after the fall of Delhi.—*Author.*

Chapter Twelve

SURGERY IN A FROCK-COAT

THE YEAR drew to its close, the Departmental Offices busy with a projected visit to Afghanistan. Mr. Herbert Edwardes was trying to arrange a meeting with Dost Mahomed, Amir of Afghanistan, but John Nicholson was dead against the idea.

"You will get no good out of it!" he said, over and over again. "Those Afghans cannot be trusted!"

Mr. Edwardes' expression softened.

"It's natural enough you are so bitter. They killed poor Alexander, I know, but that was years ago!"

"And what of my brother William? Found dead in his tent with his ribs crushed in; a mystery that was never solved!"

"You don't lay that at their door?"

"I never judge till I know the facts, but Pathans always remember a defeat. Their thirst for revenge ends only with death, and how were they to realise it was William Nicholson, and not myself, sleeping in the tent that night?"

Mr. Edwardes rubbed his chin thoughtfully.

"Well, I only hope your fears are groundless. Sir John Lawrence considers a treaty an excellent move, and is willing to meet the Amir if we can fix it up!"

"You will get no good out of it," the Deputy Commissioner turned away. "I don't want to have anything to do with such a crazy scheme!"

But as a result of their conversations, there was a great deal of extra work in the office, much wiring along the telegraph, and several journeys into the foot-hills to meet ambassadors from the Afghan court.

Christmas came, a strange Christmas among the stone courts and Hindu temples, with native life brawling along the bazaars.

"But nevertheless I am reminded of home," said Private Davies, whom Dicky visited in hospital on Christmas morning. "When I look through the window I see the great mountains all covered with snow, just as they will be in my village at the foot of Snowdon. Yes, indeed, home does not seem so far away as during those terrible hot summers. Very terrible, they are, you know. I am sure I shall be glad when I see my green valleys again!" and he sighed.

"Shall we then sing of them, Mr. Davies?" asked Corporal Alwyn from the next bed, and they broke into one of those melancholy tunes so dearly beloved of the Welsh. One by one the other inmates of the ward took up the air, till the room was filled with the throbbing music.

Dicky heard a loud disparaging sniff at his elbow, and turned to find Mr. Price gloomily inhaling a large pinch of snuff.

"Hallo, Marvel," he remarked. "Our paths cross again, eh? If an Englishman made that noise, I should be justified in concluding he was delirious.

Rum thing, the national spirit, isn't it? The Scotsman loves to make a row like a dying pig, the Irishman waves a shillelegh, while the Welshman moans and wails like a lost soul!"

But his fingers, as he took Corporal Alwyn's pulse, were very gentle.

"Hum, your fever's down. You will be able to leave here at the end of a week! And now, let's have a look at your scratch, Private Davies!"

Carefully he unwound the bandages, and bared an ugly gash high up in the fleshy part of the shoulder.

Its edges were swollen and red, but little pus had formed. Above the red ring of inflammation there was a vivid blue-green streak in the flesh.

"Why, Mr. Davies, your wound is healing beautifully," called out the Corporal. "My goodness, I remember when an Afghan shot me in the leg, the pus poured out in cupfuls! He will soon have no pain at all, eh, doctor?"

"No," said Mr. Price, "he will soon suffer no pain." He stared a moment at that ominous green streak above the gash, then carefully renewed the dressings. "And your fever has almost gone, too, eh, Private Davies?"

He straightened himself, and walked away, and later Dicky, spying him in his office, stuck his head round the door. He had been rather puzzled by Mr. Price's manner, for he knew him better than the soldiers.

"Mr. Price," he asked, "Private Davies is going to get well, isn't he?"

The surgeon stared at him owlishly over the tops of his horn-rimmed glasses. Then, very deliberately, he took a pinch of snuff.

"Oh, yes," he said in an off-hand manner, "he will soon see the green valleys again!"

"Is he going home on sick leave, sir?"

"No, Marvel," said Mr. Price. "He is going to die!"

"What, from that silly little knife stab?"

"Yes, from that silly little stab. Not because it is a wound, but because it has become gangrenous. I saw your sharp young eyes follow mine to that ominous patch of blue and green! However," Mr. Price took a pinch of snuff, "his end will be without pain!"

"But, sir," cried Dicky in great distress, "is there nothing you can do?"

"I could amputate the arm. But the gangrene would persist, and the end be just the same!"

Dicky stared helplessly at the surgeon, tears smarting in his eyes, and Mr. Price stared back at him, took off his spectacles, and put them away in his waistcoat pocket, his fingers trembling.

"Mr. Marvel," he said, his lips pursed, "during the recent campaign in the Crimea, some ghastly blunders were exposed, some of the worst in my own department. Wounded soldiers had no proper food, there were insufficient bandages and dressings and drugs, and often they had to lie on dirty straw or on the cold filthy floor. Miss Florence Nightingale, that blessed woman, stopped all those horrors. But she could not stop the wounded dying like flies in thousands from gangrene and erysipelas of their wounds, any more than the most famous surgeons can stop them dying in the hospitals at home. We don't know why the infection occurs, nor how it takes place, but we do know that the foulest wound has a better chance of clearing up than one become gangrenous. And suppuration and gangrene of wounds are allied to fevers in the system. If ever the cause of wound infection and fevers is discovered, the man who does so will be more deserving of the thanks of humanity than the whole tribe of statesmen and politicians put together! If only we knew how to avoid or control infection, there are few operations a surgeon could not perform with complete success. As it is, the interior of the body is a forbidden territory, we daren't make even the slightest scratch without shrinking from fear of what our knife may inflict. We are in fact a miserable race of humbugs; charlatans who claim powers we don't possess!"

And he got down from his stool, and began taking off his coat.

"Better run away now. I've got to take a foot off a dhoolie carrier."[1]

He indicated the little room adjoining, with walls

---

[1] Palanquin or Sedan chair porter—*Author.*

of cracked plaster and its slate-topped table. Under the table stood a large bucket of sawdust, and a bucket of grimy water stood against the wall. Other furniture there was none. Ugly blotches stained the splintered floor boards, flies buzzed cheerfully against the small tightly closed window, and on the door hung one or two rough cord tourniquets and a few dusty sponges. This was the operating theatre of the hospital, in which Mr. Price operated in a frock-coat specially kept for the purpose, and whose stains and rents indicated the experience of the wearer.

"Some of the big men in my profession have a coat so stiff with dried blood and discharges it will almost stand up by itself," Mr. Price had once said enviously to Dicky; who, as he turned away saw the surgeon take some silk ligatures from his waistcoat pocket and hold them in his teeth while he looked over his instruments.[1]

The fateful year of 1857 dawned, that memorable year of blood and fire, destined to close for ever a fateful chapter of Indian history.

In the Administrative Offices of the North-West Frontier, however, the future seemed bright and auspicious, for Dost Mahomed had agreed to meet the High Commissioner and Mr. Edwardes in the hills. A treaty had been drawn up ready for their signatures, and only John Nicholson refused to express pleasure at the success of their diplomacy.

[1] Since our grandparents knew nothing about germs, the necessity for strict cleanliness, particularly in hospitals and at surgical operations, was not recognised.—*Author*.

Four days later he rode out of the town with Dicky, an escort of fifty of the Punjab Irregular Horse clattering behind, and headed for the mountains fifty miles to the rear of the Khyber Pass, where the meeting was to take place. His eye was stern, and his expression boded ill for the Afghans should any treachery take place. As Dicky glanced back at the town, he saw a glittering procession emerge, bands playing, flags fluttering, a regiment of sepoy horse with whom rode Sir John Lawrence and Mr. Edwardes, in front a detachment of the Twenty-fourth Regiment of Foot, drums rolling, fifes squeaking, Brigadier Sidney Cotton leading them on a white horse; a colourful, almost barbaric display, designed to impress the wily courtiers of the Amir.

A hundred yards away to their right was the white man's cemetery, which six infantrymen of the Twenty-fourth Foot were just entering, two leading the way with reversed muskets, four bearing on their shoulders a rough coffin.

John Nicholson rode across to them, followed by the leading files of his escort.

"Who are you burying here?" he inquired.

"Private Davies, sir," replied the Corporal in charge. "He was knifed in a squabble at the gates!"

The Deputy Commissioner instantly saluted, and the swords of the stalwart Sikhs flashed as they presented arms.

"A lonely, forgotten grave on the frontier. The

price of duty!" said Nicholson in a low voice, and his eyes rested a moment on a headstone near the wall. Dicky, peering at it, saw it commemorated Colonel Mackesay, Commissioner of Peshawar, murdered at Peshawar in 1853.

A private lifted a bugle to his lips.

"Troop! Trot! Canter!" cried Nicholson, wheeling round his horse, and they spurred away whilst the Last Post rang across the valley to the watching hills.

Chapter Thirteen

ENCOUNTER WITH THE PATHANS

For four days they wandered through the mountains, patrolling the mountain roads by day, at night bivouacking on rocky spurs where they could not easily be surrounded during the hours of darkness. Dicky would slip stiffly from his saddle, and assist the Deputy Commissioner to dismount, whilst the bearded troopers erected his tent, and tethered their horses to their lances, which they drove, point down, into the ground. Then wood would be gathered, iron pots set simmering on the camp fires, sentries posted, and Dicky would stand by Nicholson's chair while he took his meal. As he fell asleep, the scent of wood smoke and rock herbs was in his nostrils, and overhead the sky was brilliant with stars. In the morning his companions loomed like ghosts through the mists of the dawn, and once or twice as the mists cleared, he found himself looking down into an immense gulf, out of which the thick vapour swirled like a boiling pot.

But though they met with occasional caravans, and saw one or two hillmen spying on them, all was quiet, and they rode on late one morning past three bullock carts creaking up the stony road. A solitary driver led each cart, but as the last files cantered past, a considerable number of Afghans suddenly jumped up from the edge of the road, and poured a ragged volley across the carts into the startled Sikhs.

"Do not return their fire, brothers!" Nicholson wheeled his horse and rode back to the rear, contemptuous of the balls whistling through the air. "Our mission is peaceful, remember!"

Three of the troopers were wounded, and a fourth was killed, but their comrades grimly propped them up in their saddles, and, such was their iron discipline, rode on without breaking formation.[1]

At sight of John Nicholson's formidable figure, the Pathans had scattered with shouts of alarm, but now they emerged, screaming insults after the troop and dancing derisively in the road.

"Mr. Edwardes has given us a nice job, eh, Marvel?" said John Nicholson between his teeth. "One scuffle now, and all his efforts to tie Dost Mahomed to a treaty of friendship fall to the ground. I warned him not to trust these dogs! Let's hope this business isn't a sample of what is happening to him and Sir John Lawrence!"

But two days later, they stood on the brink of a cliff that dropped away sheer to the valley below, and saw a tiny procession wind slowly along it, the roll of drums and squeak of fifes rising like fairy music to their ears. "So they have been successful!" said Nicholson, leaning forward from his saddle and peering down, shading his eyes with his hand. "And I was wrong. For once, I am very glad!"

Raising his arm over his head in signal, he gave the order to make for home.

[1] An actual incident—*Author.*

Dicky slept at night in a position of honour—rolled in blankets at the entrance to Nicholson's tent. The rustle of the boots of the sepoy posted as sentry by the door never disturbed him as he walked to and fro. On that night, however, he was painfully awakened by one of the boots thrust into his ribs, and jumped up to find it was almost dawn.

The sentry indicated two figures standing in the gloom, and bent to call softly to the Deputy Commissioner. Dicky, buttoning his jacket, peered at the strangers, who seemed vaguely familiar. Then he recognised the squat bulk of Harbans Bhandari, whom he had chatted with only the evening previous. He held by one finger and thumb, as a man holds a noxious insect, the wriggling, swearing, spitting form of Dev Sahai.

"What is the matter?" John Nicholson emerged, tugging on his coat.

"Ah, bah," Harbans Bhandari spat in the dust, and gave his captive a disgusted shake. "I was making the round of the sentries, Lord, when Fazir Khan and I heard a rustle in the grass. Then were our hearts glad, for we believed the evil ones crept upon us, and there would be a fight to take the softness from our bones, our swords would drink blood, and it would not be in shame for our gentleness we returned to our hearths. But lo, when I leapt upon the rustle, it was naught but this dirty spying brat of a thieving merchant!"

He flung his prize at Nicholson's feet, and the Deputy Commissioner hauled it upright.

"Why, I know the youth!" he exclaimed. "What are you doing here, Dev Safai? There is blood on thy robe! Is it thine?"

"Oh, Nikkal Seyn," panted Dev in English. "Some of it is, and some of it the camel drivers of my father's caravan. As we returned from Kabul we found three bullock carts lying deserted in the road. When my uncle stopped to inspect them the hillmen poured down upon us from the rocks. This was at dusk last night, and as we had seen thy troop two days gone I came to see whether I might find thee!"

"You took a risk," observed Nicholson. "It we had not been riding in a circle, we should have been thirty miles away by now, instead of four or five!"

"You know the spot where we were attacked, Lord?"

John Nicholson nodded, and smiled grimly as he called for his havildars.

"So we shall have a fight!" roared Harbans Bhandari in great glee. "Mannikin, forgive me that I almost throttled thee. Thou art as welcome as the swallow that brings a message of spring!"

And he tossed Dev into the air like a huge ball, set him carefully down, and bounded off among the startled troopers lying in their sheepskins, flourishing his sword over his head, and screeching like a madman.

As the short morning hymn of the birds rose to crescendo, they came to a sharp rise in the road, beyond which, as Dicky remembered, lay a mile-long valley, mid-way along which they had met the bullock carts.

"Ten of you, my brothers, remain here," said Nicholson, coming to a halt. "Ten to the right, and ten to the left. I and the remaining twenty will ride along behind yonder crest until we meet the road again. When you hear a shot, spur down, and spare not!"

Twenty minutes later Dicky peered cautiously over a boulder at the far end of the valley. Behind him John Nicholson sat motionless on his great charger. The sky above was a glory of pearl and rose-pink, but from the huddled victims in the road rose thick fumes from smouldering bales of goods. Camels and pack-ponies lay motionless or kicking feebly along the trail, in a welter of broken boxes and torn trailing silks. But though many of the camel drivers lay huddled with their charges, in one corner a defiant group struggled with the shouting hillmen who swarmed like ants over an upturned honey jar, stabbing and looting, whilst others poured down from the slopes, or threw their rifled treasures into the bullock carts. A din of oaths, screams and shrill cries of triumph, rose thinly to Dicky's listening ears.

"Please, sir," he said, scrambling back, and spring-ing to attention, "I think the Afghans have only just attacked again! Some of the caravan folk are still alive!"

John Nicholson nodded, and drawing a pistol from his belt, fired it into the air. Then, his eyes blazing, he dug in his heels, and galloped down to the valley, lifting his great charger over obstacles, skimming the rocks like a vision of wrath to come, while with fierce war cries his troopers flooded after him.

The Pathans looked round with excited shouts, then turned to scurry to the shelter of the rocks.

But Nicholson had swept far ahead of his troop, and was already hacking and slashing at the foremost bandits. Seeing how few in number were those that followed him, the Pathans rallied, and one or two of the more daring ran forward, crouching to stab up at his horse's belly. Dicky, who had lost one stirrup in jumping to his saddle, and was lumbering uncomfortably in the rear, thought it was the end. But out of the eddy of screaming hillmen, Nicholson's spreading shoulders towered like a crag splitting a surging wave, his arm rising and falling like a blacksmith's. To his right, to his left, he slashed, lunged at a bearded ruffian clutching at his boot, then Harbans Bhandari was at his side, and once more the Afghans scattered away for shelter. In vain; down the slopes on either side, up the road ahead, came the rest of the troop, lances in rest, a gleaming line of steel spear points and fluttering yellow turbans. No mercy was given, they trod down those who opposed them beneath the thundering hooves of their mounts, flung others aside, spitted from breast to back by the stabbing lances, or struck them senseless with the butt. With wails of terror and despair the survivors rushed madly, senselessly, in every direction, and the Sikhs leapt from their horses and dragged them down, stabbing and choking the life out of them. As Dicky galloped up, he saw Harbans Bhandari stretch out his arms, his lance dangling from its leather loop round his wrist, grab two luckless Afghans by the scruff of their necks, and bang their greasy heads together with a vicious crack. Then, dropping his lifeless victims, he jerked up his lance and coolly forked off in mid-air a screaming Pathan who leapt at him, knife in hand, from a nearby boulder. John Nicholson had sprung from his horse to attack a tall chief standing at bay against a dead camel, and Harbans Bhandari whooped with delight as Nicholson brushed aside a hillman who fired an ancient musket almost in his face, and sent him spinning into the dust with a terrible back-handed slash across the face. Then he sprang at the chief, who swung his tulwar high over his head; through the smoke resounded a dull thud; the tulwar flew into the air, and the chief, his head almost severed from his shoulders, joined his kinsman in the dust.

"That's the end, I think," observed Nicholson, removing his cap and carelessly inspecting a bullet hole through the crown. "Are any left alive, Bhandari?"

The Sikh stared round, and shrugged his shoulders expressively. Not one hillman remained on his feet, and the troopers were cutting the throats of the wounded.

"No, lord," he said in disgust. "They were but a poor lot, outnumbering us only three to one, and their hearts as water!"

"Still, you've had your revenge," returned Nicholson. "For this is the band that fired on us the other morning. I recognised the green scarf in the chief's turban. I am glad they attacked the caravan, for it gave us the necessary excuse to wipe them out. Such vermin must be taught manners!"

Dev Sahai ran forward with delighted cries, and clasped one of the half-dozen survivors in his arms.

"Uncle!" he cried, "I feared you were dead!"

"So did I," returned burly Zafar Muhamed Safai hoarsely. His eyes were red-rimmed, his beard clotted with dust and blood. "Even as the great Nikkal Seyn rode down to our aid, my sword broke off short, and I had to choke yon dog with the hilt!" He kicked angrily at a bearded hillman flung lifeless over a bale of silks. "But Allah was merciful, and thou and I art spared! We owe our lives to Him, and to thee, O mighty one!"

And he salaamed stiffly to John Nicholson.

Chapter Fourteen

MUTINY

BACK at the Administrative Offices, Dicky espied a gun of unfamiliar make lying on the Deputy Commissioner's table.

"Aha!" said John Nicholson, picking it up, and examining it with a sparkling eye. "The new Enfield rifle, eh? So at last we shall be able to serve them out to the sepoys. It's an improvement on the Minie rifle, Marvel, that we and the French used in the Crimea. You won't see the Minie, or the familiar old muzzle loading percussion rifle any more now, except in museums!"

And squinting down the rifled barrel, closely examining the firing mechanism, he walked off to discuss distribution of the new Enfield rifles with Mr. Edwardes.

Towards the end of the following week he came in and remarked to Dicky, "How would you like a holiday, Marvel? You've worked hard, and we're all very pleased with you, but all work and no play makes Jack a dull boy. Mr. Edwardes is going down to Calcutta to meet his wife, and would be glad to take you along if the idea appeals to you?"

"Yes, sir, thank you, sir," said Dicky eagerly, and stood up stiffly at attention. "But what about you, sir? I'd love to go, but——"

"Oh, Mr. Nicholson is going to have a holiday too," Mr. Edwardes strolled in from the inner

181

office. "He's going to sit here and stamp reports, and have a nice lazy time with his feet up on the table. Now we've got that old ruffian Dost Mahomed coralled at last, everyone can relax! So if you want to come along, Marvel, do so. I and my wife will be pleased to have your company!"

And so it was arranged, and Dicky rode with the Commissioner across the teeming land of India, crossing the mighty sacred Ganges at Benares, and entering Calcutta late one dusty afternoon.

Putting up at a hotel facing the Hooghly, Mr. Edwardes made inquiries, and found his wife had already arrived, and was staying with friends. Dicky was left to his own devices for a day or two, and read in an old English newspaper that Lord Canning had been appointed Governor-General, succeeding Lord Dalhousie, and was the thirteenth holder of that illustrious office. Before setting sail, he had made a speech at a farewell dinner given in his honour, at which he had observed, "I wish for a peaceful term of office; but I cannot forget that in the sky of India, serene as it is, a small cloud may arise, no larger than a man's hand, but which, growing larger and larger, may at last threaten to burst and overwhelm us with ruin."

Dicky scratched his head and stared absently at a calendar, which informed him they were in the month of February. He was rising to find out what date it was, when the door flew open and Mr. Edwardes strode hurriedly into the room.

"Marvel," he said, "do you think you can find your own way back to Peshawar? I will follow as soon as I can, but it is vitally urgent that Mr. Nicholson has these letters as quickly as possible. And before long it will be impossible to rely either on the telegraph or the post!"

"Yes, sir," said Dicky. "I know the road all right. When shall I start?"

"At once. There has been trouble over the cartridges for the new Enfield rifle. As you know, they have to be slightly oiled or greased, and some idiot of a low-caste Hindu has been spreading the tale that beef fat and hog lard are used for this purpose. All cattle are sacred to the Hindu, whilst the Mussulman regards the pig with horror, so very serious trouble may break out—in fact, it's already begun. Sepoys at Barrakpor and Berhampore have panicked, refused to return to duty, and set fire to houses, and a soldier named Mungul Pandi, one of the 34th Native Foot at Barrackpor, has fired on his white officers. It is most important that Mr. Nicholson hears of this before the story reaches the frontier regiments of sepoys. So off with you immediately. Here is money, and here is a special letter for Mr. Nicholson. If the natives collar you destroy this letter at all costs!"

Dicky had intended to visit his old friend Horace George Duff, whom he learnt had been sent from the Eighty-Seventh Foot into hospital at Calcutta. But Mr. Edwardes grave expression and anxious manner

filled him with alarm, and saluting, he ran off to
hustle his few belongings into his haversack.

For the first sixty miles or so he travelled along
the new Trunk Railway. The carriages were crowded
with chattering natives, who pointed at each other
with giggles and meaning sniggers as white officers
hurrying to their stations boarded the train at
various stops. There was a tense air of excitement
everywhere, and the few white soldiers on the stations
and in the train were rudely jostled, and their kit
broken open or stolen. At quite a few places, stones
and filth were hurled at the coaches, and through
the windows Dicky saw fakirs and Sadhus and
Brahmins—especially Brahmins—wildly harangu-
ing noisy crowds in the village streets. He was very
glad to have the company of a large and burly
trooper, whose blue uniform with red facings
proclaimed him one of the famous Hodson's
Horse,[1] travelling to Delhi after a week's leave, and
who returned the jostlings and sly foot-stampings
with compound interest, till the carriage abruptly
emptied.

As the last native limped out with baleful glares,
the trooper stuck out his elbows with a sigh of
relief, and turned to Dicky with a smile.

"Ah'm reet glad to see an honest English youngster
after all these daft fools!" he remarked. "What's
thy regiment, lad?"

---

[1] Now the 9th Bengal Lancers (blue with white facings) and the 10th
Duke of Cambridge's Own Lancers (blue with scarlet facings)—*Author*.

Dicky explained he was a civilian orderly to John Nicholson.

"Eh, then tha's lucky! Tha'll see a bit o' fighting, mebbe!"

"But don't you think the sepoys will mutiny, sir?" asked Dicky.

"Them poor creatures? What if they do? They haven't the sense to hang together! But if thou art scairt, ride along o' me to Delhi. I'd be glad o' a bit o' company—and happily we might see some junketings!"

They were destined to see more than junketings before Delhi was reached. News of the mutinies at Barrackpor and Berhampore had run, in some mysterious fashion, like a fuming powder train up the Ganges valley, and as they rode on to Patna and from Patna to Benares and Allahabad, they were more than once fired upon, from ambush and openly, by knots of insolent sepoys, drunk with bhang and rum.

At a village near Benares a mission station was blazing, and as the road dipped along the Ganges bank, they saw the murdered body of the missionary lying on the shore. They rescued a Lancashire cotton merchant from the hands of a frenzied mob led by a Brahmin whom George Procter, the trooper, kicked into the gutter; and at Allahabad got involved in a scuffle with a Sepoy picket and were hauled before the commanding officer, Colonel Simpson.

"You are a disgrace to your uniforms!" he shouted at them.

"Eh, but one of them black boys drew a knife on us!" protested Trooper Procter.

"Don't argue with me!" raved the Colonel. "How dare you insult my sepoys? I would trust them with my life!"

Dicky and his friend might have been clapped in the military prison, and slaughtered in the massacre five months later by those same faithful sepoys; only Lieutenant Brayser, who marched them away, deliberately turned his back, and gave them a chance of escape that they instantly took.

"Danged if I knaw what's come over everyone!" grumbled Trooper Procter as they once more headed north, towards Cawnpore. "Things 'ave got all topsy-turvy like, all of a sudden!"

They met with so many excited crowds in the villages, so many groups discussing affairs in the highways, bullock carts and pack-ponies pulled anyhow in the traffic, that Dicky began to wonder whether he would ever reach Peshawar at all. Twice their horses were stolen, and at posting houses where they stopped to buy corn and fodder, the natives were always slyly insolent, and even obstructive, until John Procter had rolled up his sleeves and thumped a few heads.

At length however their roads parted, and the trooper rode off after a hearty slap on Dicky's shoulder which almost broke it. Dicky paused a moment, staring after his broad back, quite sorry to lose the cheery Yorkshireman, then chirruped to his horse, and set his face to the barren plains.

After the moist heat of the valleys, it was refreshing to feel the cold wind from the hills, flecked with occasional spots of snow. But still that menacing sense of tension persisted, and as he passed caravans and Afghan pedlars, men peered up at him, muttering to themselves and clutching their dagger hilts.

Back at Peshawar he found the Administration Buildings humming with activity. John Nicholson, with a word of praise, broke open Mr. Edwardes' letter and scanned it eagerly.

"Rumour arose at the factory at Dum-dum, near Calcutta, where the cartridges for the new rifle are manufactured—sepoy regiments disaffected—regiment at Berhampore brought down under guard to Barrackpor and disarmed—Mungul Pandi—Pandi, eh, Marvel?—wounded the white adjutant and a white sergeant—hum—sepoys refuse to bite their cartridges lest they are defiled and lose caste——"

He laid the letter down, and stared across at Dicky.

"News of this business, needless to say, had already reached us, but this letter gives us full details. I've no doubt at all that it will lead to the great rebellion we have been waiting for! The reign of the British Raj shall last a hundred years—Ha! We shall see. Call the sentry, Marvel, and then I want you to ride over to the cantonments, where

you will find Brigadier Sidney Cotton, and Mr.
Chamberlain, who has recently been promoted
Adjutant-General. Give them my compliments, and
ask them and the senior officers of the Twenty-
Fourth Foot, with whom they were to dine, to step
over here as soon as convenient. Oh, and send Fazir
in as you go. I must notify Sir John Lawrence at
once!"

By the following evening John Nicholson had
already struck. The startled sepoy soldiers in the
cantonments and the town were rounded up by
detachments of the Twenty-Fourth Foot, and
disarmed under the menace of loaded rifles.

Then he rode out with Adjutant-General Neville
Chamberlain to inspect the Punjab Native Frontier
Force, who marched on to the plains eight miles from
the city, and drew up in three detachments of
infantry with the Punjab Irregular Horse in the rear.
Both he and Chamberlain recognised that news of
the insurrections in the Oudh must have already
become common knowledge to the Sikhs, and since
the cavalry were more trustworthy than the foot
soldiers, they were drawn up in the position where
a sudden charge would be most effective. Through a
drifting haze of sleet and fine rain, the two officers
walked their horses up and down the ranks, narrowly
scrutinising equipment and arms, just as in more
peaceful times, but always with a suspicion at the
back of their minds that at any moment shots might
be fired or they be cut down into the mud.

It was with a heartfelt sigh of relief that the Adjutant-General wheeled his horse out of the narrow files, and trotted with John Nicholson to a little hillock facing the troops.

"You speak to 'em, Nicholson," he said in a low voice. "These Sikhs know you better than they do me!"

So Nicholson reined in his great charger a few yards from the nearest detachment, and raised his arm high over his head.

"Warriors of a hundred battles, brothers with whom I have endured for the glory of India and the peace of the great White Queen the scorching summer suns, and the freezing mountain blasts, and ridden knee to knee, shedding my blood with yours, in a score of desperate fights, ye have doubtless heard that along the green valley of the sacred Ganges certain evil sepoys have broken their solemn oaths and rebelled. They give as reason for their black treachery that the cartridges for the new rifles are smeared with ox and pig fat, and hence are unclean, defiling a true believer. But if this were so at first, it is so no longer. I, Nikkal Seyn, your father, your friend, and your comrade-in-arms, swear by my honour that what accident did occur has already been corrected, and that your cartridges bear only a little oil of the type familiar to you for cleansing your equipment and softening your saddles and rifle slings!"

He paused and swept his eyes along the ranks.

"As ye are my brothers, whom I know I can trust,"
he went on, "I do not expect disaffection in your
ranks. Yet, if there be any who consider those
cartridges they have received have already defiled
them, or who do not believe my words, let them
leave. And the first man who steps from the ranks,"
he added with a grim smile, "I will shoot with my
own hand!"

With a flourish he drew a pistol from his holster
and cocked it.

There was a pregnant pause. The Adjutant-
General, despite the cold, felt the sweat trickling
from under his helmet.

Then a faint ripple passed over the listening Sikhs.
The foremost ranks swayed, the ripple grew to a deep
murmur, to a mighty roar of thunderous appreciative laughter. Tall bearded soldiers stamped their
feet on the earth, chuckling and crowing, nodding
admiringly at each, and pointing with shouts of
mirth at the pistol in Nicholson's hand.

"Ye are free to leave, my brothers—oh yes!—and
the first who steps from the ranks—bang!—he is
dead!"

The ground shook again beneath thundering
hooves as the Punjab Irregular Horse, swords
brandished in air, the troopers screaming fierce war
cries, suddenly broke into a gallop, and swept round
the wings of the infantry regiments to come to an
abrupt stop below Nicholson.

"All hail, Nikkal Seyn! Lead us where ye will,

mighty one! We are thine to death, to the very gates of hell!"

Sobbing like children, senior officers with red velvet facings on their blue and brown uniforms leapt from their saddles, and crowded round John Nicholson, kissing his hand, pressing his boots against their turbans. But he pushed them away gently, and, himself, dismounting, threw his arms round their shoulders, and clasped their hands.

"I thank thee, my brothers, with all my heart. But kneel not to me, who am but one of ye. Sharpen your swords to uphold the law of the weak against the strong who oppress them!"

As they returned to Peshawar, the Adjutant-General furtively mopped his face.

"I've been in some hot corners, but, by Gad, I don't want another do like that! For two rupees we'd be lying in our blood at this minute! You are a wonderful man, Nicholson!"

"Any news over the wires, Marvel?" inquired Nicholson, striding into his office.

"No, sir, but there's trouble with the 55th Native Infantry! They have refused to turn out for parade!"

"All in good time," replied Nicholson, glancing at a clock on his table. "Send Fazir in here, please! When Brigadier Cotton arrives, show him in at once!"

Settling down at his desk, he began to write a letter to the Governor-General, Lord Canning.

"I strongly advise that the Frontier be held at all

costs. Give up everything except Peshawar, Lahore, and Multan . . ."

"Here, Fazir," he said, looking up as the clerk sidled in. "Address an envelope for this letter I am writing to the Governor-General at Calcutta. Don't entrust it to the regular post-man; give it to the sentry outside. He has orders where to take it!"

Signing his name with a final flourish, he blotted the letter, and was folding it carefully when Brigadier Cotton entered.

"Sit down, Cotton, will you? I won't be a moment!"

He watched Fazir leave the room, and close the door. Then he leant forward, leaning his elbows on the desk.

"Sir John Lawrence has not arrived yet, but every hour, every minute, is of the utmost value. We must at all costs keep the border quiet. The old court of the Moghul Emperors at Delhi is the danger spot, and if the Punjab and Kashmir join the mutineers, our white troops south of Delhi will be hopelessly outnumbered, and India lost!"

"Delhi is where old Major-General Reade has dashed off to, isn't it?" asked Cotton, that wiry sandy-haired man of war.

Nicholson nodded briefly.

"Yes, he will contact Brigadier-General Wilson from Meerut with his Lancers and artillery and the other white regiments from Umballa. They are to march on Delhi at once!"

"And Dost Mahomed and his Afghans?"

"That is where you come in. In case Dost isn't sensible enough to see which side his bread is buttered, will you take the Twenty-Fourth Foot up into the hills for a show of strength? The Eighty-Seventh Foot are hurrying back, and Chamberlain will support you with the native Punjab forces!"

"Are they to be trusted?"

"I should not like to say that," John Nicholson shook his head slowly. "Some of the border horse are pure Hindus. But the Sikhs can be relied upon to the last man, I talked to 'em at a parade this morning. The best way to ensure their loyalty is to give 'em something to do! Preferably some stiff fighting, against hereditary foes if possible!"

Cotton smiled grimly as he rose to his feet.

"They'll get their fill if Dost Mahomed breaks his word! Right, I'll order the Twenty-Fourth to march at once. What are you going to do?"

"Take my Sikh horse, and disarm a sepoy regiment at Nawshahra!"

"Good huntin'," said Cotton. "Nice business, ain't it?"

"Holding down a vast province with a handful of white and Sikh soldiers?" John Nicholson laughed, "Yes, we've got a man-size job on our hands!"

Chapter Fifteen

THE CAPTURE OF DELHI

ONCE MORE Dicky got to horse as John Nicholson led his troopers out of Peshawar. There was need for haste, for at the gates they were met by a white-faced messenger, one of the two young cadets from England, reeling in his saddle from exhaustion, and gasping out the news that the 55th Native Infantry had shot their white officers, the 51st were also in open revolt, and that the 10th Irregular Horse were wavering, and would probably join them. The Colonel of the 87th had swung aside his regiment to block their triumphant, plunder-laden march from Nawshahra. Riding hell-for-leather cross country to Mardan, Nicholson found the 87th Foot almost completely surrounded, formed in a defiant square round which surged the yelling mutineers. The 10th Irregular Horse were galloping up to join the mutineers, when Nicholson and his yelling troopers fell like a hammer stroke upon their wing, crumpled them up, and wheeled to take the sepoys in rear. Already somewhat mauled by the indomitable little regiment, whom they outnumbered four to one, the sepoys broke, in vain attempting to close their ranks, for the majority, seeing who it was thundering down on them, fled in disorder. Dicky, swept along by the rush, saw dimly the red-coated square dissolve as the 87th Foot joined in the pursuit, and suddenly found Privates Murphy and O'Brien hanging on to his stirrup leathers.

"Ride him, me bucko! Ride, Dicky, kim on, we'll be the foremost yit!" screeched Private O'Brien with a wild halloo!

"Sure, 'tis the sweetest foight iver I was in!" yelled Private Murphy. "Arrah, take your hat off thin to a gintleman, ye're scrawny dhobie[1]!"

And he smote a sepoy reeling into the dust with a terrible blow on the head from his musket butt.

But, breathless and indignant, they had to fall off as John Nicholson galloped on, driving the mutineers before him, and rounding up the survivors at the Hills of Swat. Handing them over for summary justice to the 87th Foot—800 sepoys were shot or hanged—he turned and rode back again to Peshawar.

It was a sharp and bitter lesson which brought good results. Except for one other revolt at Jhelam, when the sepoys hoped Nicholson was embarrassed by plans for relieving Delhi, it was the only serious attempt at a rising in the Punjab during all the perilous anxious months that followed. And on that occasion, the sepoys made a miscalculation. They trapped and rather badly cut up the 24th Foot, but John Nicholson was in the district, swept across the Trimmu Ghat, and, rescuing the 24th Foot, caught the mutineers in their turn by surprise.

For Dicky, it was the beginning of a nightmare period of his life which ever after seemed to have the

---

[1] A native washerman of low caste—*Author.*

hazy unreality of a dream. He seemed always to be thundering in a cavalry charge, or stumbling, exhausted, after boots that rose and fell endlessly, under torrential rains or a pitiless sun that struck men down to right and left with sunstroke; whilst through rain and swirling dust resounded the rumble of cannon wheels, shrieks and groans, the deep-throated Hurrah! of a charge, and the sweet wild music of the pipes; and the scarlet coats of line regiments, the green jackets of the Rifle Brigade, the plaids and swinging kilts of the Black Watch, the blue and red tunics of Hodson's Horse, the scarlet busby-bag and black and white plume of the 9th Lancers, merged into a shifting, twinkling blur of gold and scarlet, brown and white and blue.

Back at Peshawar he heard that a mutiny of the 3rd Native Cavalry at Meerut had led to a terrible massacre. The chimes of the mission church bells on Sunday evening, calling the white soldiers to church parade, had been a signal for the regiment to break into the jail, and release eighty-five of their comrades who had been imprisoned for refusing to touch their cartridges. Their badges had been stripped from their tunics, and heavy irons riveted on their legs, but released, they took a terrible revenge. That night the streets of Meerut ran with blood. The 11th and 20th Native Infantry joined the rebels after shooting their white commanding officer, Colonel Finnis, and until dawn they raged up and down the city, dragging the white residents from their homes, murdering, looting, torturing, amid the crackle of blazing buildings and the shrieks of their victims.

John Nicholson, gathered with Sir John Lawrence, Brigadier Cotton, and the Adjutant-General over a huddle of maps and papers, struck his fist furiously on the table.

"What was General Hewitt doing?" he cried. "Meerut is the only station in India where there were more white troops than sepoys! He could have crushed the revolt with one bold blow!"

"He sat helpless whilst the residents were butchered," observed the Adjutant-General. "And during the next day, too!"

"While the rebels marched away with all their loot hot-foot for Delhi," nodded Cotton, "the danger spot of India!"

"Delhi must be retaken at all costs," said Nicholson. "I am afraid the few white soldiers there will be massacred!"

"I quite agree," said Sir John Lawrence. "Delhi is a sacred city to the Indian, with all its old traditions of pomp and ceremony. The mutineers must not be allowed to hold it for long! That is why I have been considering abandoning the frontier. Every man, every gun, will be needed to capture Delhi without delay! However, Lord Canning has wired that we must if possible hold the frontier. I believe you wrote him, didn't you, Nicholson?"

"Yes, Sir John," replied Nicholson. "Perhaps I was rather hasty, but——"

"Don't apologise," Sir John Lawrence raised his hand deprecatingly. "You only anticipated what I would have said myself. I agree it is most vitally necessary to keep the border quiet—if possible, and we can only pray to God that Dost Mahomed of Afghanistan is as honest as he appears to be. Yes, come in!" as a knock sounded at the door.

A dapper young man of twenty-five years of age entered, and saluted smartly. A faint gold moustache adorned his upper lip, his boots shone, his scarlet coat, gay with gold lace, fitted him like a glove.

"Frederick Roberts [1] reporting for duty, sir!" he said to Sir John Lawrence, and the other members of the little group rose to their feet with murmurs of surprise and welcome.

"Why, Roberts, welcome back to Peshawar!" cried Sir John. "Let me introduce our Adjutant-General, Brigadier Cotton, and Mr. John Nicholson!"

"The best gunner the Peshawar field battery ever had!" laughed John Nicholson. "I was most sorry when you left us in 1856!"

"Posted to the Quarter-Master General's Department of Staff, eh?" said the Adjutant General. "What happy wind has wafted you back again?"

"I've been posted Staff Officer to your movable column!" said Roberts, sitting down with a jingle of spurs and sword scabbard in a chair the Brigadier drew out for him. "Headquarters are expecting big

---

[1] Later the famous Field-Marshal Lord Roberts of Kandahar, V.C., K.P., G.C.S.I., G.C.I.E.

things from the officers of the Punjab, you know! Here are some despatches!"

The fuming powder train running up the Oudh, which had already exploded at Meerut, was threatening other magazines at Lucknow, Cawnpore, and Allahabad.

The sepoy regiments at Delhi had welcomed the mutineers straggling in from Meerut, and thrown in their lot with them. Only the great magazine was still held by Lieutenants Willoughby and Forest and eight white soldiers. As the mutineers fought and swaggered in the streets, murdering and looting, the white residents fled to the shelter of the Ridge, a fold of rising ground outside the city walls. In the Royal Palace lived the last descendant of the mighty Moghul Emperors, a broken old man, a pensioner of the East India Company, torn between friendship for the white people and terror of the drunken sepoys who clamoured in ever increasing numbers at his gates.

Days passed into weeks whilst the Punjab Movable Column was formed and the little group of indomitable men in the Administrative Offices at Peshawar made their preparations, and grimly watched the hills from which at any moment might pour a horde of wild tribesmen thirsty for blood and loot. Insurrections here and there were put down at once with a firm hand, and John Nicholson seemed never to sleep at all, spending long hours in the saddle, and the nights in planning and writing.

One afternoon he sat in his office with Mr. Edwardes, checking over some returns.

"Come in, Marvel," he said as Dicky appeared at the door. "Some news from Calcutta?"

"This wire just came across, sir. I can't get any reply!"

John Nicholson stared at the slip of paper, then without a word pushed it across to Mr. Edwardes.

"Sepoys come in from Meerut . . . burning everything . . . Mr. Todd is dead . . . and we hear several Europeans . . . we must shut up . . ."

It was the last wire from Delhi. The date was May 11th, 1857.

Chapter Sixteen

"SUCH A FIGHT!"

THE SEPOYS, it was learnt long after, had planned a general rising for the 31st May, but some of the regiments had gone off half-cock in their excitement. Thus the fuming powder train produced only a series of terrible disasters instead of an immense explosion in which many of the Hindu princes, notably the lesser nobles and tukaldars, had intended to join, and which it was hoped would blow the British right out of India. But the capture of Delhi fired other mutinous and semi-mutinous sepoy regiments to burst out, and few of the landowners had time to join them, though here and there were savage insurrections, the queen of the Jhansi leading her troops in person.

At Cawnpore lived Nana Sahib, a Brahmin, who, when the three sepoy regiments of the garrison revolted, took possession of the town with his force of fierce Mahrattas, and offered his palace at Bithoor as shelter for the European residents. Meanwhile General Wheeler, the English officer commanding, for some extraordinary reason abandoned the massive magazine which would have made an excellent fort, and marched his white garrison of four hundred and sixty soldiers into a hastily erected mud fort on the plains outside. The mutinous sepoys plundered the treasury, and made off for Delhi. But Nana Sahib followed them, enticed them back with a tale

of more treasure in the barracks and in General
Wheeler's new fort. The sepoys returned, attacked
the mud walls of the flimsy erection with some
slaughter of the garrison, and finally drove them in
desperation to seek the proffered shelter at Bithoor.
Nana Sahib promised them safe passage down the
Ganges, but as the weary garrison, with whom were
seventy invalids, and two hundred white women
with their children, pushed off in the boats, a
murderous fire was opened from sepoys in ambush
on both banks. Those boats which touched the shore
were attacked by other sepoys and Mahrattas. Within a few moments, every boat was riddled with
bullets, and of two that had reached midstream, only
one escaped, its thatch "awning" blazing, riddled
like a colander, rudder smashed, the blood of its
occupants staining the sluggish river. Those
that remained alive in the other craft were
dragged ashore, the wounded and many of the men
stabbed to death, while the shuddering women,
"Judy O'Grady and the Colonel's lady," and the
wailing children, were hustled off into a gloomy
dungeon. Some of the white men were blown from
the muzzles of cannon, and General Wheeler was cut
down by a brutal blow in the neck, as he climbed
out of his palkee,[1] before he had even reached a boat.
Two months later, alarmed by the approach of
General Havelock, the Nana ordered the women and
children to be shot, but even the hardened sepoys

[1] Sedan chair.

refused to murder them in cold blood. But five assassins were found, who entered the dungeon armed with glittering razor-edged tulwars. By that time, swollen by new arrivals, there were over two hundred women with their children crammed into the dungeon, and all were killed, slaughtered like sheep under the flailing swords of their murderers. It was dusk before the last pitiable victim was cut down. Next morning the bodies were removed, stripped, and thrown into a well; a ghastly tale of black treachery and savage cruelty that appalled even those Hindu princes who favoured the cause of the mutineers.

Under Dicky's startled gaze, the stammering morse key of the telegraph jerked out many another story of grim disaster, of bloodshed, and deathless heroism.

At Delhi, Lieutenant Willoughby and his tiny band defied swarming hundreds of sepoys battering at the gates of the magazine. As one by one the gallant eight white soldiers fell, and sepoys appeared over the walls, Private Scully hurled a flaming torch into the magazine, which exploded with terrific force, killing most of their assailants, though of the garrison Lieutenants Willoughby and Forrest escaped, scorched and blackened, to their comrades on the Ridge. At Lucknow, Sir Henry Lawrence, elder brother of Sir John Lawrence, and who had recently been appointed Chief Commissioner of the Oudh, grimly kept the city from breaking into open revolt, though the sepoy regiments were mutinous, and had refused to surrender their arms. They bided their time till other mutinous regiments from the Eastern Oudh had time to join them. On the 30th May the Residency guard rushed up to the Residency, where Sir Henry sat at dinner with his staff. As they drew up in line outside, he quietly stepped on to the veranda.

"Shall we load, lord?" cried a havildar derisively.

"Yes, let the men load their muskets!" replied Lawrence.

He stood awaiting their volley, but his obvious contempt disconcerted the rebels. After a few tense moments they turned and rushed away into the darkness, whilst Sir Henry coolly resumed his dinner.

More than once the stuttering line died abruptly, and Dicky knew that it had been cut. Yet after a few hours it would begin to transmit again, and he remembered how he had seen carried into the hospital a mortally wounded sapper who had given his life to repair the line; clinging to a telegraph post, a splendid target for sepoy sharpshooters.

But into Peshawar were pouring tall bearded Sikhs, clamouring to recruit in the Punjab Column, and day after day detachments of sturdy Ghurkas and Rajputs tramped in from far Kashmir under command of their white officers. Prince Seth Premchand of Mangrulkar rode in with two hundred picked horsemen, every one of them a seasoned warrior, and there were many other nobles and squires who brought money or jewels, or men, to swell the munition chest and the army of the great Nikkal Seyn.

Dicky, standing in the bazaar as a long column of stocky Ghurkas filed through the town to the cantonments, overheard an officer of the Twenty-Fourth Foot remark to a brother officer junior in rank:

"It is a lucky thing for us that John Nicholson has been on duty here the last few years! If it wasn't for the affection these natives have for him, the border would have been ablaze weeks ago!"

"Oh, yes, jolly good show, what?" The ensign snatched despairingly at his monocle, and made another determined attempt to screw it into his round china blue eye. "But what about Edwardes and his jolly old treaty with Dost Mahomed? What?"

"Oh, I'm not denying that that was an excellent move. But a treaty with the Amir—even if he'd kept to it—wouldn't have been much use with the troops of the Punjab and Kashmir joining the mutineers! No, when the history of the Mutiny comes to be written, John Nicholson will be proclaimed the saviour of India!"

"By jove, how frightfully excitin', what?" The ensign sighed as the monocle once more escaped from its moorings.

At last preparations were complete. John Nicholson had succeeded Adjutant-General Chamberlain as Brigadier-General of the Punjab Frontier Force, and

Lord Canning, who had acted with admirable speed, and had already sent for white regiments from Rangoon and England, ordered Sir John Lawrence to dispatch a force immediately for the recovery of Delhi.

"And I'm delighted that you have been placed in supreme command," wrote the Chief Commissioner. "There is no man in India more fitted for the post!"

So with a siege train, four regiments of Ghurkas from Nepal, the Punjab Irregular Horse, some regiments of the Punjab native forces and a seasoning of white soldiers, John Nicholson led the way out of Peshawar, Dicky riding with Harbans Bhandari in the ranks.

On the 28th June the Punjab Movable Column left Phillaur for Amritsar, arriving there on the 5th July. A sepoy regiment had mutinied at Jhelam, massacring their white officers and many other Europeans. John Nicholson promptly took some of the Punjab Irregular Horse and rode after them, catching them at Trimmu Ghat, and pursuing them with great slaughter across the Ravi river. Returning to join the column at Amritsar they marched on to Lahore. The beleaguered camp on the Ridge outside Delhi, ringed in by thousands of bloodthirsty mutinous sepoys, was reached on August 14th.

"Ai!" remarked Harbans Bhandari thoughtfully. "'Tis not the first time I have seen Delhi, but never did I dream of viewing it with such great happiness. Look how the evil ones swarm on the walls!" and he drew out his sword, "Have you a whetstone, youngster? Some excellent blood-lettings impend, I swear!" and as Dicky handed him a stone, he set to work to improve the edge of his tulwar, which was already razor-keen.

"Hallo, youngster!" hailed a familiar voice. Mr. Price sat down with a groan beside Dicky, and tenderly nursed his feet. "Who's your ferocious friend? Some one has taken a nasty chip off his alae!"

"Off his what, sir?" inquired Dicky.

"Nostrils, boy. Where's your education?" The surgeon took a pinch of snuff. "Crowded round here, ain't it? Women and babes in arms, camp servants and soldiers, cannon and feeding bottles—reminds me of August Bank Holiday on Hampstead Heath, except for the guns, of course. Smells like a Bank Holiday too! I'll bet you a rupee to a blood orange we shall have some pretty cases of cholera before long!"

Day and night the luckless garrison on the Ridge were exposed to constant fire from the sepoys. As more and more mutinous troops poured in, their fusilade grew incessant, and casualties correspondingly higher. In order to stop further reinforcements reaching the Ridge, the mutinous sepoys began skirting round the flanks, marching and wheeling with an orderly precision that brought gloomy approval from the white officers who watched them.

"They don't forget what we taught 'em," grunted one, squinting through a telescope. "Makes me groan to think of the hours I spent training the beggars!"

The regular army officers were a little contemptuous of the semi-military officials of the East India Company, but they soon forgot any jealousy as they realised what a born leader of men the new Commander was. Rallying whole-heartedly round John Nicholson, they gave him every assistance as he began to lay his own plans for meeting this dangerous threat in the rear.

"And it won't be too soon!" grumbled Harbans Bhandari as a six-pound cannon shot rumbled through the air and smashed his cooking pot into a whirl of flying sparks and cabbage. "This is not war! It is a game of skittles, where we are the pins!"

But on the afternoon of the 25th August he swept out with his yelling comrades as Nicholson suddenly struck at the mutineers who had completed their movement, and were massing behind the shelter of two boggy marshes across the river Najafgarh.

It was a bold and risky action on the part of Nicholson, but he had selected the critical moment when, one manœuvre completed, the sepoy regiments were in temporary confusion as they fell into line for an intended attack on the rear of the Ridge.

The sight of the huge figure on the great black war horse caused more confusion. Though the havildars[1] and other officers stood firm, many of the rank and file began scurrying about like ants, until the shouts of their comrades made them realise what excellent shelter the marshes provided. Amid a steady downpour of rain they hurried to deploy along a front of two miles, extending from a canal to the little town of Najafgarh, and posting a battery to command the bridge across the river.

Dicky, jolting along knee to knee with the eager Sikhs, peered through the slashing rain to see the green oozy fields disappear behind clouds of white powder smoke. Whilst foot soldiers opened out along the river banks to the left, returning the fire, Nicholson thundered on, mud flying shoulder high, leading his men to a deep ford. Dicky was so wet, the prospect of plunging into the warm muddy stream did not bother him, and he was moreover fully engaged in controlling his horse. Bullets were humming round like vicious bees, and the Sikh troopers jostled him out of the way. He found himself, finally, galloping madly up a path along the edge of the river, the nearest troopers some yards away, yelling exultantly as they waved their lances at the sepoys on the farther side of the ford.

"Whoa, you brute!" screamed Dicky. "Not that way, you idiot!"

Desperately he tugged at the reins as the path plunged into a dense clump of bushes and mango trees, and almost shot out of the saddle as two

[1] A native Sergeant of our Indian infantry regiment—*Author*.

natives ran to meet him, and the startled horse reared and slipped backward.

"Hold him, Dicky!" shrilled a familiar voice. "Catch the reins, Dev!" boomed another voice in Hindustani.

Dicky, gasping and blinking, clambered back off the horse's neck to stare into the face of Dev Safai, who grinned back at him. A few yards away his uncle Zafar flourished a tulwar and strutted proudly up and down the path, his portly figure crammed into a worn uniform splitting at the seams.

"We've brought your drum, feringhee!" screamed Dev through the crash of musketry and the deafening roar of the cannonade. "The revolt has stopped all trade, so we came to help! But we were cut off by the sepoys, and have lain hidden in those bushes for two days! Uncle put on his old uniform—it's a bit small for him now, eh?" and he darted back to the trees, and returned proudly carrying the battered drum of the 87th Regiment of Foot.

"No more talk!" roared Zafar Muhamed. "On, on to battle!" He danced impatiently in the path, flourishing the tulwar over his head.

"But—can he—can you—swim the ford?" Dicky shrilled back. "Here, let him ride, and you and I will cling to the stirrups!"

And he made signs to Zafar, who with an amused laugh and an approving pat on the shoulder, leapt into the saddle, and thundered down to the river, Dicky and the Indian youth rushing after him.

The mud was trodden into slippery grease, and smeared with blood. As Dicky clung wildly to the stirrup he had grabbed, Dev clutching like a leech to the other, he lost his footing entirely, and the river closed over his head. Spitting out a mouthful of mud, he came up choking, the drum however was held by Zafar, and was still dry.

Up the opposing bank they rushed, and Dicky hastily grabbed the drum and let go as Zafar lifted the horse over the groaning forms that strewed the fields. Nicholson had hurled his troopers against the left centre of the enemy, and they were locked in a savage mix-up of darting lances and stabbing bayonets. But slowly the sepoys were giving ground, though Dicky could see nothing through the choking powder smoke and the flying hooves of the cavalry. A lane slowly opened through the struggling ranks ahead—the sepoys broke, some running back along the river bank, towards the bridge, whilst a larger number strove to close their ranks against the searching lances of the exultant Sikh troopers. Dicky, stumbling over the bodies on the trampled earth, had one glimpse of John Nicholson, his eyes blazing, wheeling at the head of his men, then the fight shredded away, and staring round he saw Zafar Muhamed shouting at him, pointing with his reddened sword to the bridge half a mile away. It bristled with cannon, many of which the gunners were even now training on the Punjab Horse.

"Those cannon will cut them down like ripe

corn!" yelled Dev, rising from beside the body of a sepoy who had snatched at him as he lay in the mud, and whom Dev had promptly banged on the head with a broken musket butt.

At once Dicky saw what he must do. Bending low against the bullets whistling overhead, he ran, as he had never run before, down the river bank in wake of those sepoys making for the bridge. The ground shook as two horsemen galloped madly after him, Zafar Muhamed and Harbans Bhandari.

When he was clear of the wild struggle in the paddy fields, Dicky stopped, and pulled the drum into the correct position. As his fingers clutched the sticks, and he paused for one moment motionless, he saw Harbans Bhandari and Zafar rein in their horses, and lean from the saddle to embrace in farewell. Then his wrists flickered, and across the marshy wastes, through the hissing rain and the crackling musket volleys, there burst out the stirring notes of The Rally!

A dull Boom! Another, and another, rumbled like distant thunder from the batteries at the bridge. Shot and shell whined and roared overhead, bursting with dull thuds and a fountain of mud. A twelve-pound cannon ball slithered into the blood-soaked earth only a few yards from Dicky, plastering him from head to foot with slime, whilst those sepoys who were making for the bridge paused, and dropped to one knee, firing with their muskets, the nearest making for Dicky and his two guardians with shrill screams of rage. Harbans Bhandari with a defiant yell cut two of them down with one stroke, but Zafar Muhamed tumbled to the ground as his horse was shot beneath him. Then they were swept up by a maddened mob of terrified fugitives, who strove vainly to stamp them down and stop the warning thunder of the drum.

At last one sepoy, grinning with rage, broke past Zafar Muhamed, and lunged at Dicky with a gory bayonet. He skipped aside, and continued madly to beat The Rally! The Rally!

But the Punjab Horse had heard its warning notes at last. With a great shout, they wheeled and poured like a pack of hounds upon the batteries, leaping over the rough earthworks and sabring the gunners, the sepoys running up behind them till the fields were filled with a milling circus of struggling men. John Nicholson appeared to be in a dozen places at once. Wherever a few sepoys sought to make a stand, he would charge out of the smoke, hacking and thrusting, his yelling Sikhs jabbing with their long lances, till at last the whole left centre lost all formation, and ran with despairing cries from the marshes, carrying away in their confusion other regiments which still maintained formation.

By dusk the whole Sepoy force was flying for its life, 6000 men routed by little more than a fifth of their number, John Nicholson taking many prisoners all of whom he hanged, all of the baggage, and thirteen guns.

It was the last attempt made by the sepoys to crush their defiant enemies on the Ridge. After such a disaster, they learnt caution, and shut themselves up within the safety of the strong fortifications of Delhi. The road was now open for reinforcements to pass unchecked to the Ridge, and the telegraph and other communications were restored. One of the first messages received was from Sir John Lawrence, who telegraphed to Nicholson from Lahore, "I wish I had the power of knighting you on the spot. It should be done."

But as the din of the pursuit died away across the river, Dicky, his wrists aching, laid down the drum, and walked over to where Harbans Bhandari lay prone, his battered head pillowed on Zafar Muhamed's arm. Zafar's own tunic was in ribbons, and blood trickled down into his beard from a long gash across his temple; but Harbans Bhandari had been run through the body as he leapt from his saddle upon a sepoy officer who had that moment pistolled his horse. Now his great chest heaved with shuddering gasps, and a cold sweat stood upon his forehead.

"It is—good to die—among friends," he whispered, and smiled up at Dev who had squatted down at his side. "Ai, I am glad to have seen—such a fight! Where—where is—my young, white brother?"

"Me, sir?" squeaked Dicky, his eyes filling with tears.

"Aye, thou art—our brother—gallant was your act. Give me—your hand! So! Give—my love, young feringhee—to Nikkal Seyn—ask him—not to forget—my son!"

The rain had ceased, and the sun shone through the mists.

Harbans Bhandari lifted his arm, and strove feebly to salute. Then his body suddenly relaxed, and with a deep sigh he fell back in Zafar's arms.

"Dead?" whispered Dicky.

Dev nodded slowly as Zafar bent his head and cradled the dead warrior in a silent ecstasy of grief.

Chapter Seventeen

"TILL DELHI IS TAKEN!"

SUPPLIES and reinforcements poured in, until over 15,000 souls were gathered on the Ridge and the neighbouring cantonments, which had been abandoned by the sepoys. This number included women and children and camp servants, as well as fighting men comprising the Punjab Movable Column, the 52nd[1] and 61st[2] Regiments of Foot, Hodson's Horse, the Carabineers[3]—young soldiers mounted on untrained Australian "walers," hastily assembled to replace a regiment sent to the Crimea—and two troops of European artillery under command of Brigadier-General Wilson from Meerut, and who shared command of the operations against Delhi with John Nicholson.

To the south of the valley of the Ganges and Jumnha was hidden beneath dense clouds of rolling powder smoke. The Residency at Lucknow was besieged by thousands of mutinous sepoys, and Sir Henry Lawrence had been mortally wounded by an eight-inch shell which burst in his office. At Allahabad, Colonel Simpson, on June 6th, had addressed an evening parade of his sepoys, thanking them in glowing terms for their loyalty, and reading to them the formal thanks of the Governor-General

[1] Now the Oxfordshire Light Infantry.
[2] Now the Gloucestershire Regiment.
[3] Now 16th Dragoon Guards—*Author.*

for their offer to march against the mutineers. Within four hours, seventeen of his officers and many women and children had been massacred, and he himself severely wounded. Now he held out with a few Sikhs in the fort, whilst fierce Colonel Neill turned from suppressing a mutiny at Benares to march at head of his famous "Lambs"—the 102nd Foot—to their relief. Beneath the blazing sun, many of the "Lambs" fell dead from sunstroke, and Neill himself only kept going by having buckets of water constantly poured over his head. Sir Henry Havelock had been recalled, and with 1500 men set out to rescue the victims of Nana Sahib's treachery at Cawnpore. He was opposed by Tantia Topi with a large army, and successive defeats did not drive him from Havelock's path, who at last arrived at Cawnpore only to find the women had been massacred; and joining up with Colonel Neill and his regiment, marched to Lucknow, forty-five miles away, only to be besieged in his turn.

The fate of the British trembled in the balance, and John Nicholson saw that at all costs Delhi must be recaptured. But Brigadier-General Wilson pointed out that there were nearly 4000 cases of cholera in the camp, and that they had insufficient artillery.

"We can never hope to batter down those massive walls," he said. "And if we make an assault and are beaten back, we shall be surrounded again."

"Then we must get the sappers to blow breaches at given points!" cried Nicholson.

The very same night he went down alone into the dry ditch surrounding the city walls, and until dawn walked round the defences. The following night he actually scaled the walls, and entering the city, made notes of the sepoys' positions. By some extraordinary piece of luck, on this occasion he met not a single sepoy, although he deliberately walked among the cannon of a battery he saw was held by Sikhs. The drowsy sentries thought he was a ghost, and threw themselves flat on their faces, moaning with terror.

"Oh, shameless ones!" hissed Nicholson. "Dogs, snakes that strike at a defenceless heel! What do ye here when thy brothers are without the walls?"

"Lord," they wailed. "We were captured, and two of us tortured before the rest, till we agreed to serve the guns!"

"Then get back to thy brothers, who keep faith!" and as they rushed away, he ran softly after them, driving them over the walls with his cane.

Primed with his new knowledge, he urged once more that an attack be made without further delay. Brigadier Wilson was ill with fever, and at first obstinately refused to discuss the matter further. But his officers, fired by Nicholson's example, argued and expostulated, until at last he shrugged his shoulders, and gave in with an ill grace.

"It is your pigeon, Nicholson," he said. "I refuse to take any responsibility for such rash actions!"

So the few guns possessed by the besiegers were brought up, and began a cannonade intended to distract the sepoys attention from Nicholson's real purpose. The sepoys returned the fire with vigour, and day and night shot and shell tore into the wretched white folk, who had no cover at all. It was the monsoon season. There were fierce drenching squalls of rain, while the temperature in the shade was always over 100° Fahrenheit.

"Hi, Marvel," called Mr. Price one day, as Dicky passed with a message to the gunners, "come and give us a hand when you're finished. I've moved this blessed hospital tent four times this week, and every wretched time, only a few hours pass before those sepoys get the range. They've blown us up once, as if this mud isn't trying enough!"

To Nicholson's delight, the bombardment by the European batteries proved surprisingly effective, and breaches were smashed in the nearest walls. Four columns were formed, each of about a thousand men, Nicholson placing himself in command of Column One. With each column was a party of sappers carrying bags of gunpowder to make further breaches.

On the evening of September 13 Dicky stepped out of his tent, where he had been helping Nicholson draft some reports and despatches, and stood staring through the orange dusk at the great city below. A faint haze of dust and smoke hung over its broad avenues lined by trees, its roofs and minarets, while the rays of the descending sun gilded the flat roof of the Diwan-I-Am, or Hall of Public Audience, with its sixty pillars of red sandstone, the white marble pavilions of the Imperial Palace, the lofty Kutb-Minor tower, five stories of graceful alternating red sandstone and marble, and the massive battlement of the ancient Shajahanabad, the fort built by the Emperor Shajahan, rising along the placid waters of the river Jumna for a third of the city's river front of two and a quarter miles. The complete circuit of the city walls was five and a half miles, and along its whole length swarmed the mutinous sepoys, puffs of white smoke from the batteries mottling the parapet, while a dull noise of thousands of voices rose like the murmuring of bees.

"A fine sight, eh, Marvel?" said John Nicholson, stepping out of the tent. "The great city of Delhi, seat of the old Moghul Emperors, the spiritual Mecca of every Indian! To-morrow it will be ours! You must come with us and bring your drum!"

"You sound very confident, sir!" Staff Officer Frederick Roberts cantered up, and briskly dismounted.

"Of course I am! I've got plenty of men, and excellent officers. I owe you, particularly, a debt of gratitude for talking Brigadier Wilson round!"

"It was fortunate I was posted to the Delhi Field Force, as Deputy Quarter-Master General with the artillery against Delhi," returned Roberts with a twinkle. "If I'd still been with your column, he probably would not have listened! But he couldn't very well snub his chief artilleryman!"

"Are you coming into the town to-morrow?" inquired Nicholson.

"If I can manage it, I shall be with your column! But I'm afraid I may be kept back until later!"

During the hours of darkness four sapper officers crept down into the ditch to examine the breaches already made, and reported that they were practical for storming. The four columns were assembled, and stood at ease awaiting the dawn.

Slowly the gloom lightened. A grey streak appeared and widened across the sky, and the stars grew pale. Dicky, standing by the leading files of the 52nd Regiment of Foot, saw the motionless figure of John Nicholson, statuesque on his great charger, grow more distinct and sharp. An infantryman coughed, and his sergeant swore at him softly. Then the sun rose into the heavens, a flaming ball that changed into a blazing disc of gold. As the first warm rays struck down to the earth, John Nicholson raised his arm high over his head! It was the signal for the attack!

There was one short roar of cheering, then the ground shook as the columns broke into a double, and rushed madly for the walls looking out of the mists.

There were answering screams of rage and alarm from the sentries on the parapets. Mist and walls were blotted out as with a deafening crash batteries opened fire, and storming shot cut red lanes through the advancing files.

But the breaches were already reached, and a fierce hand-to-hand struggle began in the gaps. More and more of the attackers rushed up, leaping over the crumpled bodies of their comrades, while from every angle a deadly hail of shot and shell was poured upon them.

Nicholson, raging in the van of his column, had struck spurs into his charger, and skimmed like a swallow over the shattered masonry into the city beyond. For a moment he was alone, but as, striking madly to right and left with his tulwar, his horse was shot from under him, the first infantrymen of the 52nd Foot tumbled in, their officers yelling "Tally-ho! Gone away!" and the snarling sepoys were swept back to the streets. Column two had also forced its breach, and was slowly, relentlessly, fighting a road through. Near to Nicholson, Column Four had found their gap too high to scale, so made a daring attack upon the Kashmir Gate. Led by Lieutenant Home, a dozen sappers, each carrying a bag containing twenty-five pounds of gunpowder, rushed across a beam thrown over the ditch, and flung down the powder before the gate. Then they jumped clear into the ditch whilst the firing party raced up. Lieutenant Salkeld fell, shot through the arm and leg, but as he dropped, handed the port-fire to Private Burgess, who was shot dead. Sergeant Carmichael, who had been laying a train, grabbed the fire from Private Burgess, lit the fuse, and in that moment collapsed mortally wounded.

But the powder exploded with a deafening roar, the column swept through the gate, and rushed into the streets to join Nicholson and his men. A ghastly struggle began as the grim-faced storming parties met with increased numbers of sepoys pouring up from their barracks. Column Four had been unable to find a breach at all, and after some desperate attempts to scale the thirty-foot walls, had fallen sullenly back, leaving a trail of dead and wounded; the three columns that had gained entry were outnumbered ten to one.

Dicky had run, till he felt his heart would burst, with the cheering infantrymen, scrambling in over broken masonry which barked his shins and scraped the skin off his hands and elbows, to find a savage hand-to-hand fight swirling up and down those streets which led to the walls. Sweating, shrieking sepoys were dragging up light pieces of artillery to blast away their impudent foes, and John Nicholson ran suddenly up a staircase that led from the Kashmir Gate to the parapet of the walls.

Dicky turned to follow him, wildly beating out once more "The Rally! The Rally!" but at that moment one of the light guns fired.

It had been hurriedly aimed, and the ball did no execution, striking high up on the wall by the staircase. But it dislodged a fragment of stone and brick already loosened by the explosion at the Kashmir Gate. Down it rumbled, striking Dicky's shoulder, pitching him headlong forward across his drum, which was shattered by his weight. Sick and dizzy, he found all power had gone from his right arm, whilst his hand was pinned beneath the masonry. And there he lay in a kind of swoon, fortunately shaded by the wall, listening dully to the groans resounding round, until three hours later a familiar face was poked into his ashen features.

"Tck! Tck!" said Mr. Price, beckoning the hospital orderlies who accompanied him to lift aside the rubble. "It's young Marvel. Now what have you been up to, eh?"

His voice and hands were as gentle as a woman's.

"Not—gangrene, sir?" whispered Dicky.

"Good gracious me, no," smiled the surgeon. "A broken collar bone and a green-stick fracture of the upper arm! We shan't need to use the knife at all— you'll be as right as a trivet in a month!"

Meanwhile Nicholson had stormed through the sepoy ranks, the gasping storming parties ever at his elbow, until two-thirds of the wall had been swept clear. But at the Burn bastion they came to a halt. Two pieces of cannon stopped the advance up a lane from the Lahore gate. Time and time again Nicholson led a wild charge into the very muzzles of the flaming guns. Time and time again his men were shot down, although a lucky answering shot put one of the cannon out of action. His eyes blazing, mad with fury and excitement, Nicholson was rash and impetuous, and failed to realise in the heat of battle that the bastion could have been stormed with

ease had they broken through the walls of the mud
houses on their left.

"One last charge, my men, and that gun is ours!"
he roared.

But the panting, sweating men, who so far had
gallantly followed wherever he led, were exhausted
by the desperate fighting beneath the blazing sun.
For a moment they faltered, and John Nicholson ran
up the street, then paused, turning to face them,
taunting them, swinging his tulwar high over his
head.

At the very moment his body was exposed, a sepoy
saw his opportunity, aimed, and fired. The heavy
ball struck Nicholson's mighty chest with an audible
thud, entering beneath his armpit to bury itself in
his right side.

The shock of that dull blow galvanised his men
into action. Up the lane they rushed, screaming
with fury, reached the battery, and hammered the
gunners into red pulp, then fell, raging like wolves,
upon the surrounding sepoys, who fled helplessly
before them.

As they tore past Nicholson, an officer paused to
ask:

"Are you hit?"

"Yes, yes," said Nicholson impatiently, irritated
at such a senseless question, then propped himself
against the wall, grinding his teeth with fury as he
sank slowly to the ground.

"Let me get you under cover, Nicholson," said

Captain Hay, kneeling down beside him. "Hi, you dhoolie carriers!"

Four coolies approached nervously, and Nicholson was carefully lifted into their sedan chair.

"I shall remain here till Delhi is taken!" said Nicholson through clenched teeth.

Captain Hay stared at him, then nodded slowly, and ran after his men.

The coolies looked at each other in bewilderment, and then glanced after Captain Hay. With a shrug of their thin shoulders, they dumped their passenger carelessly down, and went off to look for plunder.

"You dogs!" muttered Nicholson. "You would not have dared to treat me so had I not been helpless!"

In the afternoon Frederick Roberts came up the lane, and paused to look into the sedan. With a shock, he realised the wounded bleeding giant within was the great John Nicholson, and hastily called a sergeant of the 61st Foot, who collected four privates who tenderly bore away the stricken soldier.

A surgeon who examined the wound pronounced it fatal. Fierce fighting was still in progress in the city, and he lay in a rough tent, lighted by a solitary candle, deserted and alone, attended only by some Multani natives, who jabbered outside until he cried to them to stop. For a little while they did so, then began again, whereupon with a bitter effort he picked up a pistol that lay by his bed, and fired it through the tent walls. The hint was unmistakable; after that there was peace.

"You see, Marvel," said Mr. Price, describing it to Dicky long after, "the musket ball was still lodged in his chest. If we only knew what causes wounds to go bad, and could control pus formation, we could have operated and taken the ball away. It would not have been a difficult operation. But as it is, we couldn't, and so he lingered on, growing weaker and weaker, having terrible, exhausting attacks of hæmorrhage. I've seen some sad sights in my time, but never one so pathetic as the picture of that huge giant lying there in his stuffy tent, his face ashen, great rings round his eyes, the terror of the Punjab, the greatest man India has ever known—and it's bred some gallant fellows—struck down and utterly helpless, with not one of his friends near him. For they'd all gone on into the city, you see! But it was typical of the man that when he heard Brigadier Wilson was considering abandoning the town, he took up a pistol, and threatened to shoot him if he did—aye, and repeated over and over again, "If I live, the world shall know that Alexander Taylor— the engineer who helped make the breaches in the walls—took Delhi! Always thinking of others and of his duty—that was John Nicholson!" and Mr. Price took a pinch of snuff and shook his head sadly.

John Nicholson was shot on the 14th September, and died on the 23rd. He had not completed his thirty-sixth year. Among his last words were:

"Tell my mother that I do not think we shall be unhappy in the next world. God has visited her with great affliction, but tell her she must not give way to grief."

Sir John Lawrence burst into tears when he heard of Nicholson's death, declaring, "As long as an Englishman survives in India, the name of John Nicholson will not be forgotten," while Mr. Edwardes wrote:

"John Nicholson was the brother of my public life—never, never again can I hope for such a friend—Nicholson was the soul of truth."

On the morning of the 24th of September, 1857, the body of John Nicholson was born on a gun-carriage to a new burial ground opposite the Kashmir Gate and the breached walls he had been the first to ascend.

The evening previous there had been something approaching a mutiny among the 52nd Regiment of Foot.

"Please sir, are we going to Mr. Nicholson's funeral?" asked a private, stepping from the ranks as the regiment was dismissed after evening parade.

"Certainly not!" snapped the Colonel.

"We shall go whatever you say," returned the private quietly, and every man of them did.

The fall of Delhi broke the back of the mutiny. With their sacred city firmly held by the feringhees, the mutinous sepoys and their supporters lost heart. It remained only for Lucknow to be relieved by Sir Colin Campbell after a desperate struggle before the Secundrabagh, a heavily fortified square, in whose

walls a breach was at last made. Among the first to
leap through the breach was Horace George Duff,
Dicky's friend, who had been caught up by the 93rd
Regiment of Foot[1] as they passed through Calcutta.
It is curious that in the wild rush of brawny Scots
and yelling Sikhs a drummer boy should have had
the honour to be the first. Frederick Roberts tells
how he found his dead body just inside the breach;
"a pretty, innocent-looking fair-haired lad, not more
than fourteen years of age." The last descendant of
the Moghul Emperors was captured by Major
Hodson of Hodson's Horse, and Nana Sahib fled, no
man knows where, though it is said he was lost in
the vast jungles that shut off Kashmir from Nepal.
In Central India Sir Hugh Rose stamped out the last
embers of revolt, but the East India Company was
dissolved. Their government passed to the Crown,
and on the 1st November, 1858, Queen Victoria issued
a famous proclamation to the Chiefs and Princes of
India. "We hereby announce to the Native Princes
of India that all treaties, engagements made with
them by or under the authority of the Honourable
East India Company, are by us accepted, and will be
scrupulously maintained, and We look for a like
observance on their part. . . . We hold ourselves
bound to the natives of our Indian territories by the
same obligations of duty which bind us to all our
other subjects, and those obligations by the Blessing
of God we shall faithfully and conscientiously fulfil."

[1] Now the Argyle and Sutherland Highlanders—*Author*.

One of the last acts of the Company was to award John Nicholson's mother a pension of £500 per annum. Queen Victoria caused it be known, too, that had he lived she would have awarded him a K.C.B.

As there are peasants in India who believe that the Great White Queen Victoria yet lives, so tales of Nikkal Seyn are still told along the border. He has passed into a legend with other heroes of antiquity.

And sometimes in the stillness of the hour before the dawn, the awestruck watchman on his tower in the hills believes he hears in the wind whispering down the valley, a rattle of hooves as John Nicholson once more rides through the mountains he knew and loved so well.

THE END